Mask of The
Highwaywoman

NIAMH MURPHY

Produced in the United Kingdom for NIM Publishing

First Published 2012

ISBN-13: 9781521056547

For Louise ...

ACKNOWLEDGMENTS

I would like to thank Freya Publications for their help in support with a first-time author

I would also like to thank all those fans of the AcademyOfBards.com: without such a supportive group of readers, I never would have finished this book.

ONE

The carriage charged along the road.

The sun had fallen some time ago and the passengers were shadows in the moonlight.

They should have arrived in Harrow for four o'clock, but Evelyn was beyond worrying. She let her head rest against her seat, her eyes closed, as she concentrated on breathing and tried to ignore the nauseating motion of the carriage.

The stagecoach had departed Cambridge on time and, to Evelyn's relief, it hadn't taken too long for the inane chatter of the passengers to die away. It wasn't until they reached the inn for lunch that there had been any sign of a delay.

At the time, she had been thankful for a longer break—it gave her stomach time to settle—but after several hours of waiting without news, everyone had become increasingly impatient and she had been worried she would miss her connection. When their journey eventually resumed, it was clear that what had been unpleasant was now unbearable.

All she wanted was to reach Harrow, find a nice room with some good food, rest and sleep and forget about today. Then she could start the journey afresh in the morning. Her father need never concern himself of her troubles, but she would make a note to listen to his advice in future and take their own carriage on long journeys.

She hated sharing a carriage; she had hoped it would give her a sense of independence and freedom. But instead, she was squeezed on a seat between a snoring old man and a woman with a whimpering child. The heat was oppressive, even after the sun had gone down, and the airless stench made her feel light-headed, worsened by the constant juddering of the uneven road. Their delay gave licence to the driver to speed along the highway, ensuring his passengers were shaken around, like dice in a cup.

Suddenly the coach lurched backward. Evelyn screamed as she was thrown from her place. The side of her head whacked against a hard surface and she fell to her knees in a heap of other bodies.

"What happened?"

"Is everyone alright?"

Frightened voices cried out in the chaos. The baby was screeching as its mother scrabbled around in the darkness.

Evelyn tried to pick herself up and find her bearings. Someone had landed on her foot, she was struggling to move and her head was starting to pound. There were arms and legs everywhere, clambering and pushing, everyone trying to find space where there was none. She tried to free herself from the mayhem but the more she tried to move, the more restricted she became, and she started to panic.

She tried to reach for the door or the window: she needed to get out, needed to move. She had to know what was going on, what was happening outside; she wasn't sure she could cope if the carriage started moving again.

There was shouting, angry voices on the highway.

There were always stories about what could happen on these roads after dark; she'd heard about the type of people who wandered around at night and what they might do to those they came across.

Suddenly the door was wrenched open.

A man stood, silhouetted in the door frame. He wore a tricorn hat, a mask, and a great black coat. His beard was huge and, as he grinned, one of his teeth glinted in the lamplight. He waved a musket at the startled passengers and spoke in a deep, guttural growl.

"Everyone out!" he barked.

The passengers muttered between themselves as, one by one, they descended the carriage steps. The father of the crying child stopped to help his wife and then offered a hand to Evelyn, who took it gratefully. She held on to the door frame to ease herself onto the road, she was still wobbly and light headed, and felt relieved to have the cool air on her face and solid ground beneath her feet. But her stomach turned with the thought of what could happen next.

"Come on, come on."

The highwayman herded the passengers to the edge of the lane. Evelyn glanced back at the carriage; the terrified driver sat with his hands held aloft, as a thin highwayman on horseback aimed a pistol squarely at his chest, laughing raucously. A third highwayman was manhandling the other coachman, threatening him with a blade and rummaging in his pockets.

"Everyone sit!"

It was a woman's voice.

Evelyn spun round, startled. Standing at the edge of the road, with a pistol in each gloved hand, was a highwaywoman. She too wore an eye mask and tricorn hat, with a long, black coat, hanging open to reveal a tight fitted waistcoat and breeches. The clothes clung to her body, tailored and tight fitting; they revealed every curve of her figure.

Evelyn had never seen a woman dressed in such away, she stared at her, fear replaced by curiosity.

"I said sit," the woman repeated, stepping forward.

Evelyn was exhausted from the long day's journey: her bones ached from the constant shaking of the stagecoach, her head hurt from the whack she'd received when she was thrown from her seat, and she still felt woozy and light headed from the airlessness of the compartment. She needed to stretch her legs and breathe in the cool, clear air; she couldn't face the thought of sitting on the ground and was worried that if she did, then she may not be able to get up again.

"I'd rather stand," she replied wearily. "It's been a long day."

The highwaywoman was taken aback, her mouth fell open slightly and she stared at Evelyn.

Their eyes locked.

For a moment the woman didn't move, the pistols

remaining firmly raised; she was fierce and commanding. There was strength and intimidation in the way she stood, something Evelyn had long wished for in herself—this woman embodied power and masculinity yet retained beauty.

It was intriguing but disconcerting.

She had no idea what this woman was capable of. Despite her anxiety, something in the deep recesses of her mind told her not to be scared, but she knew there was nothing to justify this instinct.

"This isn't a picnic," the woman said, finally. "I'm telling you to sit."

She gestured to the ground with her pistol and, reluctantly, Evelyn eased herself down. Her muscles were tender and sore from hours spent sitting in the same position and she struggled to reach the ground with any grace. As she was trying to find a comfortable position on the cold, hard, earth, one of her fellow hostages turned to her.

"That was foolish," he hissed. "You'll get us all killed."

She looked at him, surprised by his candour. In normal circumstances, she would have accused a man such as him of impertinence for daring to speak out of turn to one of his betters. But in this case, she realised he was probably right, and simply nodded in agreement.

She decided to try being inconspicuous. If the gang were left to go about their business then there was a good chance no one would get hurt and they would be allowed to go on their way without further incident.

She thought about how she might describe each of the men—there was no law preventing highway robbery after dark, but her status might be enough to induce criminal proceedings and she wanted to be sure they punished the right people. But in the poor light, with hats and masks, she could do little more than keep a mental note of their respective heights.

She glanced back towards the woman at the edge of the woods. First to her boots—black, with silver buckles and spurs, tapering in at the ankle and tight around the calf.

Suddenly she felt as though she shouldn't be looking and returned her attention to the passengers gathered around her, quietly comforting one another as they waited desperately for the experience to end.

Yet she felt drawn to the woman, compelled to look again, an irrepressible desire to glance sidelong at the woman just a few feet away. She was fascinated by the breeches that hugged her thighs, the waistcoat, pulled tight around the curve of her waist and the shirt, open at the collar.

Suddenly she realised the woman was watching her. Her stomach flipped as they stared at one another. She wanted to look away but she couldn't. She was transfixed.

Evelyn had never seen a woman like this, a woman who had taken her life into her own hands and was living by her own rules, who rejected what was expected of her and went her own way regardless of the consequences. She felt a pang of jealousy, but also desire: a desire to know more about her, to understand how and why this woman could have come to be.

She heard a shout, and the moment was gone as their attention was pulled back to the carriage. The highwaymen were ransacking the luggage and they had clearly found something exciting in one of the trunks. The thin highwayman was stood in the lamplight, laughing at the larger of his comrades who was holding up a woman's nightgown to himself. Evelyn groaned and prayed it wasn't her trunk they were rifling through.

Her eyes were pulled back to the highwaywoman. Evelyn wanted to know more about her: she needed to know who she was and whether she was as cruel and villainous as her comrades, or whether she was she just carefree and seeking adventure; a dashing heroine or a lowly, greedy whore.

Evelyn couldn't help feeling it was the former. She imagined this woman held a passion for freedom and had succeeded in obtaining it. But she wanted to be sure, wanted to be certain of this woman's nature.

She had a sudden urge to pull off the mask, convinced that if only she could see behind it then she would know everything about her, and prove that a woman could disregard rules and yet retain decency.

She held back, forcing her fanciful notions aside, but unable to quash the desire to at least speak to her, to press her and see what discoveries she could make.

"How much longer?" she asked.

She heard the other passengers quietly shushing her and knew that she was being a fool: she was risking her safety on a whim. But she couldn't shake the feeling that the woman wasn't dangerous. She stood, separating herself from the other hostages, and stepped closer to the highwaywoman.

"How much longer?" she repeated, but only loud enough for the highwaywoman to hear.

She stared back at Evelyn, her gaze unflinching, as she considered her answer.

"Just sit down," she said finally, with more irritation

than anger.

Part of Evelyn wanted to sit down, the same part that was always wanted to keep out of trouble, to keep quiet and polite. The part of her that wanted to please others, to never make a fuss, to timidly put up with whatever life threw at her and to consistently comply with other people's expectations of how she should behave. But seeing that woman—wielding pistols, wearing breeches, leading a group of ruffians to hold up a carriage in the dark of night—gave her the courage she needed to speak her mind.

"I would simply like to know how much longer you intend to hold us captive here," she hissed, as commanding as she was able. "We are all cold and tired, the child especially, the journey took twice as long as it should have done. I haven't had anything to eat for hours. I don't know where I am going to sleep tonight. I am meant to be in Bristol by this time tomorrow and I have simply no way of getting there—"

"Then it doesn't matter how long we take, does it?" the woman snapped. "Now," she said. Her voice was low and full of menace as she clicked back the flint on her pistols. "Sit down or I'll make sure you never stand up again."

Perhaps she was mistaken.

Perhaps she should go back and take her place with the others, stay quiet with her head down and accept that she was wrong, that this woman was as villainous as the others and she'd lost her honour when she took up arms.

But then she noticed something, a flicker of the eyes as the woman glanced at the baby and Evelyn felt the urge to push her advantage.

"That child is freezing," she whispered. "It won't cope

with much more of this."

She'd pushed too far.

She knew she'd crossed a dangerous woman, already irritated by her persistence. She wanted to take back the words, to pluck them out of the air and ram them back in her mouth. But it was too late, the words had been said and a ball of fear was starting to swell and twist in the pit of her stomach.

But then suddenly the highwaywoman lowered her pistols, placing them back into the holsters at her waist, and, with a flourish, she removed her long black coat, placing it around the mother and child, before returning to her position and raising her pistols once more.

"Now sit," she said.

But Evelyn was happy to, she felt victorious, as if she had revealed something secret. She wasn't in the presence of a typical rogue this woman was different. This woman was the way the ballads depicted: the dashing and chivalrous hero, made more enigmatic by her femininity.

Evelyn knew people would be talking of this highwaywoman; she would be celebrated for her grace, and renowned for her deeds. People would wonder at the truth behind the woman and Evelyn would know that she had seen it, had witnessed the good in this woman, she might even testify to her good honour when she was caught. Now that would cause a scandal.

"Thank you," whispered Evelyn, wanting to show that she too was capable of unexpected courtesy.

She resumed her place on the hard, dirty, earth track, satisfied for the moment that she had learnt all she wanted to know.

But as minutes rolled on, she found her thoughts

returning to the highwaywoman. She still wanted to know how this woman had come to be here, how their paths had crossed in this way, why a woman who seemed so well spoken had landed on the wrong side of the law, whether she was a victim of circumstance, or had chosen her own path.

She looked at the woman again and felt sure that someone so strong could never be a victim of anything: she had to be there by choice. But what choice, what kind of an adventure, would be so tantalising as to entice this woman?

"Right, you lot." It was the thin highwayman; he stood over the passengers, scanning their faces. "One at a time. You first." He pointed his pistol toward an elderly man, who rose clumsily. The highwayman grabbed his arm and dragged him over to the light of the stagecoach lamps, where the other two waited.

The old man was roughly searched and his pockets were turned out. Evelyn gasped when he was thumped across the head for taking too long to release a watch chain from his button. When they had taken everything of value, the old man was forced into the carriage and the highwayman sauntered back to the passengers with a grin, and pointed to the man who'd helped Evelyn down from the carriage.

"You next," he said.

One by one, the passengers were relieved of their valuables and tossed back into the stage coach. There was nothing gracious about the manner in which they were searched. They were man-handled, pulled about, and their clothes ripped, as they were shoved up against the carriage.

Evelyn looked away but she could still hear the thud of

their bodies against the solid wood of the carriage door, their yelps as they were punched and thrashed by the masked men. Evelyn stood in disbelief, the romantic tales of the charismatic highwayman fading as she was forced to witness the systematic beating of the hostages and waited for her own turn.

She glanced back at the highwaywoman, who was watching the scene impassively and Evelyn tried to fit the two people together, the woman who had wrapped a cold child in her own coat and the woman who permitted this brutality.

"How can you do this?" Evelyn asked, feeling somehow betrayed by the woman she had only just met.

The highwaywoman looked across at her. Evelyn had expected, or rather wanted, to see some sign of shock, or remorse, as if she hadn't known that the men would do this, as if she was just an innocent, a bystander in what was happening. But instead she steadied her jaw and lifted her chin, resolutely.

"The pay is good," she said, then turned back to watch the men throw the last of the passengers into the carriage, and Evelyn realised, with dread, that she was next.

The woman pushed a pistol into the small of the back and led her forward. As she came into the light of the stagecoach lamps, she looked upon the face of a highwayman. He was the shortest of the three, but he loomed over her; his skin was rough and pock marked, his smile uneven through a lack of teeth, and the ones that were left jutting out of his jaw were brown and misshapen. His blue eyes stared out from behind his mask; they were misted over, ghost-like, and she wondered if he was close to losing his sight. When he spoke, his breath was foul enough to make her retch.

"Give it up, pretty one, or Johnny here will search you himself."

He waved his pistol towards another man, half concealed in shadow: it was the man who'd opened the carriage door and herded the passengers on to the road. He was the tallest of the three, a huge man with broad shoulders and a thick wiry beard. He grinned, showing several gold teeth intermingled with the brown, and Evelyn shuddered at the thought of his hands coming anywhere near her; massive, filthy hands, shoving her and groping her until he had taken whatever he wanted. She dreaded how far it may go, and hoped that there was sufficient money in her purse to satisfy them enough to leave her unscathed.

He saw the look of fear on her face and started laughing. The others quickly joined in.

As she handed over the only money she had with her, Evelyn felt disgusted and enraged as well as frightened. The cash she had on her person was her only hope of gaining passage home, of finding a place to rest and food to eat. They hadn't just taken her money, they had taken her freedom, her independence, and her safety.

She felt violated and abused by the lowest, basest, thieves, the pestilence of the road. Vermin, swimming in filth, achieving nothing but through violence and intimidation, snatching scraps from decent people, people who deserve their rank in society. These brutes were cowards, hiding behind masks and muskets, and she would do everything within her power to see them hang for their crime. All of them.

"And that," said the highwayman, as he reached out to

grab her locket, the locket she had loyally worn every day since receiving it, it hung inside her bodice so that the heart of gold fell against her own.

Instinctively she pulled back.

"No!" she gasped, horrified and angry at the thought that he would take it.

A new sense of defiance coursed through her veins. She wasn't going to let these filthy dogs win, the locket would just be their trophy of her defeat and she was dammed if she was going to let them have it.

"Hand it over," he growled, a knife suddenly in his hand and aimed at her throat. It wasn't just his breath that stank, he was saturated with the stench of sweat and horse manure; it oozed from his tattered clothes, greasy skin and the slimy mop of hair protruding limply from under his ill-fitting hat.

Her courage was sapping from her, yet she felt compelled to deny them success, of at least preventing them having this one victory.

"No," she repeated, but her voice was unsteady. "It's of very little value, my shoes cost more." She hoped that by appealing to his sense of value it would give her some opportunity to gain ground.

"Well I'll 'ave your shoes an' all if you don't hand it over."

He stepped forward and she let out a shriek as she fell back. She was grabbed by the highwaywoman, who held her tightly around the waist and stopped her from falling, or running.

The man laughed as he watched her struggle, but the woman's arms were surprisingly strong; she couldn't break free, she would be held tight until they had finished with her.

From somewhere in the back her mind she remembered hearing about a woman who'd swallowed a ring to prevent it being taken by a highwayman, but instead of letting her go, he'd sliced open her belly to retrieve it.

Evelyn wished she hadn't spoken, she wished she'd let him have the damned locket, it was only her own arrogance and pride that had prevented it. He was always going to take it, only now he'd likely slice her throat for the insult.

"Let her keep it," the woman said.

Evelyn was stunned.

The highwaywoman was stepping in. It made no sense; she had been so callous, watching impassively as they beat the others, why was she stepping in now? What had changed?

It didn't matter: Evelyn was safe, and suddenly the arms around her waist were no longer threatening, but comforting, protecting her from the man with the blade.

"Keep it?" he asked. He briefly glanced back at his larger, bearded cohort, who appeared to be enjoying the scene. "This is the job we came to do," said the highwayman, raising his voice as he turned his attention back on the woman, "or have you forgotten that?" His face contorted with rage, and the knife in his hand was waving dangerously close to Evelyn's face.

She felt the woman's grip on her waist tighten further and the fear that had faded so quickly came back just as fast. She was caught within a feud she didn't understand and she felt as though her life was hanging in the balance, only she didn't know what weights were being used.

"It's just a chain," the woman said, but her voice was weakening, she had lost the authority she'd had and Evelyn wondered why she had stepped in to defend her, what she had risked and who was in control.

"I'll be the judge of that," said the man, before he struck Evelyn hard across the cheek with the back of his hand and wrenched the locket from her neck.

"Deal's a deal." He grunted and shoved her, unceremoniously, back in the carriage, where she fell to the floor as the door was slammed behind her.

Niamh Murphy

TWO

"So 'ave you worked in a pub afore?"

The landlord stood behind the bar, a greying apron tied awkwardly around his ample frame as he wiped a clean tankard with an old cloth. He was very much at home in the grimy tavern, as if he had always been here, decaying amongst the detritus.

Evelyn, however, was not at home. She took to the pub like a duck to a pony trek. She was clearly out of place here amongst the pub goers, in a dingy little public house. She was self-conscious, her travelling dress and cloak were delicate and refined in comparison to her surroundings; she was distinctly overdressed and squirmed as the landlord's eyes carefully took her in.

"I'm a fast learner," she said quickly, "and I have undertaken housekeeping duties for a vast estate (which was not entirely inaccurate), so I have a very good understanding of how things are run. Bedsides it would be for just one day, until I can contact a relative that lives in London."

Evelyn gave her most dazzling smile but the landlord merely stood, looking at her, his face unmoved as the slow motion of wiping the tankard continued.

After the robbery, it had taken a while for the travellers to get themselves going and it had been long after ten by the time they arrived in town. Most of the passengers had been able to go straight home, however Evelyn had to try to hunt for a place to rest.

She'd had to drag her trunk along the road, hoping that someone would take pity on her and offer her credit for the night. However, she had been turned down again and again and again and she'd quickly had to lower her expectations with regards to the standard of her accommodation.

It had been unsettling, to say the least, to wander around an unfamiliar town at night. She had been here before of course, but only when travelling, so she'd never stayed long, and only ventured into the one place, usually for a meal and nothing more. She didn't know how far she had walked, it must have been miles, round and around, up and down the same streets again and again, each time being forced into a lower and lower establishment.

She had been sure a few times that she was being followed, it was difficult to tell when the streets were so dark, but she felt certain that someone was waiting for their opportunity to take advantage of her troubled state. The last thing she wanted was to have to spend the whole night in the open: the very thought terrified her.

It was nearly closing time when, finally, her arms aching from carrying and pulling and dragging the trunk, her feet sore and swollen from walking up and down along the cobbled streets, her body so exhausted she felt she could sleep where she stood, she relented and pushed open the door to the 'Red Lion'. It was the saddest, dingiest, and dirtiest of all the taverns in town.

There was the same stench of cheap ale and pipe smoke here as there had been in all the other public houses, but this place was darker with fewer candles burning and no fire in the grate.

The patrons were few, just a couple of old men sitting alone and one large woman with a pipe, sitting beside the grate warming herself by an imaginary fire. They turned to look at Evelyn as she struggled through the door, but they barely reacted to her presence and went back to their drinks and pipes, none of them offered to help, but she hadn't expected they would.

The landlord looked up at her in surprise, it wasn't usual for a young woman of status to be wandering around late at night on her own, let alone walk into his establishment.

Evelyn wouldn't normally reduce herself to even sharing pleasantries with such a man, but now she was forced to do whatever she could to gain his favour.

She had explained her story as he stared at her, unmoved, and ready to solemnly shake his head when she asked for charity, but he looked genuinely surprised by her suggestion that she should work for her night's rest.

All she could do now was wait.

Ordinarily she would have tried to conceal her desperation, but she was too exhausted to care. She simply did her best to maintain her dazzling smile and prayed that she wouldn't have to walk any further, that she wouldn't have to hunker down in the street and beg for the money to pay for her passage home. She tried to think of a plan, about where she could try next, but she didn't know—she was alone, and without money. She was destitute.

"Just one night," he said cautiously. A wave of relief washed over her, and she could have cried with gratitude. "And it's only cause it's late and I've got an empty" he continued, putting away his tankard and reaching for a key from under the bar.

He didn't offer to carry her trunk, he simply turned and walked through a swinging door. She assumed she should follow and grabbed the handle of her trunk, dragging it along the floor in pursuit.

He was already making his way up a dark and narrow staircase and she struggled to clamber up the steps behind him.

Although the bar had been unpleasant, the smoke had clearly masked the worst of the smell: in the back-stairs there was the stench of meat just on the turn, and she was sure they weren't too far from a privy. She tried to be thankful and not to let her distaste show, but she needn't have concerned herself; he was paying her no attention at all as he barked orders to her.

"Food is extra, coal is extra. If you break anything, smash anything, tear anything, you pay for it." He led her along a narrow corridor, to a small door at the end of the hall. As he placed the key in the lock, he turned back to her. "Is all that clear?"

She nodded, with her best attempt at enthusiasm, and he swung open the door for her to consider the tiny little space that was to be her home for the night.

She had to stifle a gasp. Although she had seen the rest of the tavern she still hadn't been prepared for the condition of the room—she wouldn't have kept her horses in such a state of disorder and misery.

There was a distinct smell of damp and burnt ash, although there was barely any light she could see that the room contained a small wooden bed, covered with an old, raggedy, woollen blanket. There was a rickety chair and a small chest of drawers that she doubted she could fit her gloves in, and on the far wall was a tiny rattling window with a loose lock, which seemed to let more air in than it kept out. The walls were bare, apart from the timber frames, but there was at least a small fireplace which added a touch of cheer in an otherwise bleak atmosphere.

"It's lovely!" she said, smiling at the landlord as he handed her the key and turned to go.

"You can do your own fire I take it?"

He didn't wait for a response and disappeared back down the hall as Evelyn slowly closed the door behind him.

She locked it and placed the key on the side table, sighing to herself before getting started on the fire.

There was a small box of matches left on the mantelpiece. The box was slightly damp, and she didn't hold out much hope for the matches. She looked around the room for another, but in the semi darkness she could see nothing. She hadn't made a fire in years.

After her mother died, the house had been in such chaos and disarray that she had often been forced to light her own fire and her father had banned the servants from his chambers, so it had usually been left to her to make sure he kept warm. But at the time she'd had proper kindling, and dry matches, and light.

Her hands were cold to the bone, and her muscles were so exhausted they were shaking, the muscles in her leg twitching, unused to exercise. Carefully, she built the fire with an odd mixture of logs and sticks. The first few matches died immediately and a few more snapped before one sparked. Once she had lit a piece of kindling she had to carefully nurse the fire into life, and it was a long time before she was able to feel warm enough to take off her travelling cloak.

Finally, at rest, with her greatest worry off her mind, she tried to think about her next concern: food. With no money, she would have to rely on the landlord to provide her with breakfast, and she wasn't sure if he would. She was already hungry; she would be worse in the morning and she wasn't certain that she would be able to carry out a day's work without food, and as a result the landlord may refuse to accept her efforts as sufficient payment for the room.

But she still had her trunk. Perhaps they hadn't taken everything.

She knelt and opened the case. Rifling through the dresses, no longer neatly folded, there were a few pieces of lace which might be worth something, but she wasn't sure where she could go to sell them, she couldn't possibly give them her real name, if anyone discovered that she had been selling lace in Harrow the gossip would be all too humiliating. But her jewellery, her money, even a pack of cards she had brought in Cambridge, had been taken.

She stared down at the disordered clothes, she told herself it wasn't so bad, that she had a place to stay, some hope of getting some money to pay for a carriage home. It wasn't so bad.

But her head sank into her hands, the exhaustion and despondency grabbing hold of her. She cursed the people that had done this to her.

She cursed the callous men and that demon woman who had forced her into this situation, through their wretched, indolent gluttony.

But as the image of that woman came back into her mind, the anger dissipated. Maybe she was wrong about her: she had tried to stop them taking the locket, and the woman had held her, protected her. She remembered the arms held tightly around her waist and the desire she'd had to sink into them.

She shook the memory from her mind, cursing the woman for the effect she had. It was that woman's fault she was in this situation.

She dug around in her trunk, pulling out her night things. It was getting late—even if she had nothing to eat, she could at least ensure she had a good night's rest. Her fingers were still cold and stiff, and her muscles ached; it took an extraordinary amount of effort for her to remove her clothes and change into her night things.

But when she eventually sat down on the edge of the bed, she was unable to consider sleep; her mind was racing. She had to think of a plan to get home, and get home quickly. She only had this room for one night, so she would have to travel tomorrow, unless she was able to sell her lace, which may just give her enough money for either another night's rest or a carriage to Bristol but nowhere close to enough for both. By the time, she finished working to pay for tonight's lodgings it would be too late to find a carriage, so she would have to use the money to pay for another night. But then she would have nothing left to sell to pay for her journey.

She groaned in despair at the predicament.

Suddenly there was a rattle behind her.

Swinging round she looked at the window. The blackness beyond was empty but just for a moment. A masked face appeared.

Evelyn gasped.

THREE

She grabbed the poker and turned to face her attacker. The window was thrown open. A cold wind made the fire dance as the highwaywoman clambered through the small frame into the bedroom and carefully sealed the window behind her.

Evelyn stared at her, speechless.

The highwaywoman stepped forward.

"Don't come any closer!" Evelyn warned, brandishing the poker. She was astonished that the woman had returned, that she had the temerity to chase down her victims in order to wreak further havoc upon them. Evelyn was livid, but also frightened: she had considered her ordeal to be over and now here it was again, looming in the shadows. "You've taken everything I have, and if you touch anything else I swear I'll—"

"I'm not here to take," said the woman, softly cutting Evelyn off and raising her hand, as if to a spooked mare. "I'm here to give back." She reached into her waistcoat and pulled out the locket, holding it up for Evelyn to see the little gold heart twinkling in the firelight.

She didn't know what to say, or how to react. She stared at the woman, open mouthed. Wondering why she had come back to return the locket, why she had stepped in to try to stop them taking it in the first place. Evelyn realised it must have been the woman following her earlier, tracking her and waiting for the ideal moment to corner her, only to return what had been stolen.

"That's all I wanted to do," said the woman as she placed the locket on the small chest of drawers and backed off.

"No, wait!" Evelyn couldn't let her go. Not after this. She had to know why, she had to understand her and understand why she had come. Nothing about this woman made sense, from the clothes she wore, to the way she spoke and the actions she took. Everything was a contradiction, nothing made sense, and yet… she was akin to a magnet, drawing Evelyn closer and forcing her to want to know more. "Why did you come here?"

The woman glanced back at the necklace and then to Evelyn. Her chestnut brown eyes were soft in the firelight. She took a while to answer, and when she did her voice was slow and gentle.

"I could tell it was important to you."

Evelyn relaxed a little in her presence, and then cursed herself for it. She tried to remind herself that this woman had also compromised her security, threatened her with pistols, stolen from her and stood idly by as she was struck across the face; the force of that blow was still stinging her left cheek. She wasn't going to give the woman the satisfaction of appearing grateful, especially when she knew there was no doubt her privacy had been violated.

"Did you read it?" she asked, waving the poker in an attempt to appear menacing.

The woman didn't answer.

"You did, didn't you?" For all her attempts to appear gallant, the woman was still willing to open and read the contents of a locket never meant for her eyes. It only confirmed Evelyn's opinion of her as a dishonourable harlot.

"Evelyn, I—"

"So, it's 'Evelyn' now, is it?" She could hardly comprehend the audacity needed to utter a name acquired through such base means. She felt violated and trespassed upon, this woman had indeed invaded her privacy—she had stolen from her, threatened her, read her locket, followed her through the streets and broken into her room. Evelyn wanted to challenge the woman, to take back any victory she had gained through wrongdoing.

"How do you know the name in the locket refers to me?" Evelyn wasn't quite sure what effect she'd imagined having with this question: shame, confusion, embarrassment. Whatever reaction she'd expected, it hadn't been relief.

"You mean you're not 'Evelyn'?" the woman said, with a trace of hope on her voice.

Evelyn wasn't sure what to say. She'd wanted to disconcert the woman, to throw her off balance and regain some authority. She wanted to take back control and show the woman what was really meant by the term 'betters'. Instead it was she who was wrong footed.

Even outside of her own surroundings and faced with someone wielding a weapon, the highwaywoman seemed naturally in command. Evelyn felt herself envious of the woman's power, envious but also enamoured by it.

"Well I… I do happen to be called Evelyn, yes. But that isn't the point," she managed to stammer. She couldn't bring herself to lie, not even now.

"What is the point?" The woman looked at her, clearly puzzled by the turn their conversation was taking.

Evelyn wasn't used to confrontation, or having authority. Even when dealing with the servants she had trouble coping with errors or mistakes and would usually leave that sort of thing to the housekeeper to resolve. But she didn't want this woman to depart thinking that she had somehow alleviated her guilt: she had still stolen from Evelyn, and bringing back the locket wasn't nearly enough to absolve her.

"Did you bring my playing cards back as well?" Evelyn said, trying to regain her authoritative tone.

"No. I'm afraid I couldn't." She looked away. The woman seemed genuinely pained at her failure, and Evelyn felt a sudden pang of guilt for having caused the pain. "But I did bring some of your money back!" she said, as if just remembering. The woman removed a small purse from her coat and threw it on to the chest of drawers next to the locket.

Evelyn stared at it for a moment as she lowered her poker. She hadn't considered that she would bring money back. The woman must have known how much trouble she was in; that must be why she had been following her, not to cause more trouble, but to ensure she was safe, to make sure that she would have a place for the night and complete her journey. Then when she discovered she was in trouble she came to help, came to give back what was stolen.

Perhaps the stories hadn't been exaggerated; perhaps there really were chivalrous outlaws, ready to protect the weak, ready to leap in and rescue those in need. She would be able to get home, she would be able to pay for her night's rest; she had been saved from humiliation, saved from destitution.

"Get the first carriage out in the morning." The woman's voice was tinged with anxiety and Evelyn was surprised at her tone as well as the order. She hadn't intended to do anything but get the first carriage out; she wanted to be free from this town and as far away from this mess as possible.

"Thank you," she said, stepping forward and picking up the purse, wanting to confirm that it was real.

Suddenly the woman was no longer the villain that had robbed her in the woods; she had become a heroine that had leapt through the window to rescue her. Evelyn looked at her as she smiled, a beautiful honest smile, with soft reddish lips and her deep, dark eyes, almost infinite, behind her mask. Again, she felt the urge to see her without it, to know what lay behind the mask of the highwaywoman, she wanted to reach up and pull it from her face.

"I should go," the woman said, turning, "I'm sure there are search parties on the lookout for me this evening."

She couldn't go. Not now. Not when Evelyn was so close to understanding her, to finding out who she was, to seeing behind that mask. She couldn't let her disappear into the night, to become an ethereal, half remembered dream.

"Why did you do that?" Evelyn still held the poker, and hoped that the threat of the weapon would keep the woman here long enough to answer her questions, to reveal what kind of a woman she was, and to answer for her actions. The woman turned back and Evelyn felt her heart leap slightly as their eyes locked.

"I told you," she said. Her voice was slow, soft, enchanting. Evelyn was drawn in by her words. The highwaywoman moved closer and Evelyn didn't back away, she yielded to the desire. As their bodies moved closer she felt herself wanting to sink into the woman and be held by her once more. "I could see that your locket was important," she said, "and I was sorry." Her hand drifted up towards Evelyn's cheek, she stroked the skin delicately with her fingers, sending a thrill of excitement through Evelyn. It shocked her.

She snapped her cheek away and backed off.

"I meant why did you rob me in the first place?"

Evelyn didn't understand what was happening to her. She didn't understand why this woman was having such an effect. She looked at her with confusion and distrust. She felt a desire she'd never had before and knew this woman was responsible for it, had somehow tempted her.

She knew about temptresses, of course she did, but she'd never believed such a power was real, that such a desire could be caused. She was determined to ignore it, to overcome it, to defeat it.

But the woman didn't look evil. She looked surprised, hurt even. This only served to enrage Evelyn further, making her even angrier at this woman's ability to pull, so easily, on her heartstrings.

"You scared all those helpless people?" she said, her voice rising in anger, anger at the woman and anger at herself for being so easily hoodwinked by a thief. "That child could have died of the cold and that poor old man…"

"Oh," she said. "That."

"Yes that! As if it isn't hard enough getting by in this world without people like you riding in and taking from those who can barely afford—"

"That isn't true," she said.

Evelyn rounded on her, furious that she should dare to deny what was so obviously true.

"So, it wasn't you gallivanting in the woods with your band of merry men?!"

"Keep it down!" The woman said, glancing at the door nervously.

"Keep it down? Keep it down? I have a good mind to hand you in myself!" she shouted. "There is likely fifty pounds on your head and I know some people that could do with the money!"

"You won't hand me in," said the woman, still calm and in control despite being shouted at and threatened with a poker.

Evelyn hated her in that moment. She hated her for not being afraid, hated her for not believing the threats to hand her in and, most of all, she hated her for being right.

"Won't I?" Evelyn asked, haughtily. But she knew she had no authority in her voice, and she was embarrassed and ashamed that not only did this woman have complete control over her, but she knew it.

"No. And I do not take from those who can't afford it. Only those who travel in the luxury of a stage coach."

"You wouldn't call it luxury if you had to travel in one."

The woman laughed.

It was sudden, unexpected, Evelyn hadn't seen her laugh before, it lit up her face, it was a beautiful, untainted laugh. It cut through Evelyn's anger and she realised how absurd she must look, angrily waving her poker in the air.

This woman had stepped into help her, had brought back a sentimental necklace, and returned the stolen money when she needn't have done either. At each step she had helped, and Evelyn had thanked her by shouting at her and threatening her.

"Possibly not," the highwaywoman said, "but I am sorry you were hurt."

Evelyn lowered the poker. The woman did seem genuinely upset, genuinely sorry that she was hurt and Evelyn realised that she wasn't a harlot, or a temptress, or a callous rogue, she was just someone that had come to say sorry. But seeing this new side made Evelyn even more curious, how could one woman be so many different things, so many contradictions. She was an outlaw, a thief, a highwaywoman and yet she wasn't any of those things at all.

"Who are you?" she asked at last.

The woman smiled, but it wasn't a smug or self-satisfied smile, it was sad. She shook her head slowly.

"I can't tell you."

Evelyn couldn't let it drop that easily, she couldn't let this mystery slide away from her. She had to know who this woman was—she couldn't let her go without knowing.

"Why not?" she asked indignantly. "You know my name, why can't I know yours? Or see your face for that matter?"

She shouldn't have asked to see her face, she'd pushed too far. She could have pushed for a name, but removing the mask was too much, now the woman would leave, she'd leave and Evelyn would never see her again, never know who she was, never know why she made her feel this way.

But suddenly she took off her coat and hat.

Her clothes were tailored and hugged her figure. Evelyn noticed she wore her pistols in holsters on either side of her waist, as well as a short sword at her side, and felt stupid for having believed the poker was any kind of a weapon against her.

Slowly the highwaywoman untied her mask.

Evelyn held her breath, her whole body waiting for this revelation.

Then the mask was gone.

Evelyn stepped forward impulsively, seeing the full picture for the first time. The soft angles of her cheekbones, the way her dark hair framed her face, the arch of her brows above those deep, dark eyes.

She had expected a slightly older woman, older than herself at least. But instead she was greeted with young girl. Not a crook, not a villain, not a temptress, just a girl, a beautiful, innocent, vulnerable girl.

"All is revealed," the girl whispered.

"Not quite all," said Evelyn. Spurred on by her success and seeing that the highwaywoman was younger than she thought, Evelyn had the confidence to push for more.

The girl raised her eyebrow: she clearly wasn't sure

what was being asked of her.

"I want your name," Evelyn repeated.

"Oh…" The girl shook her head. "I really can't. I mean I shouldn't even be here, I—"

There was a trace of fear and panic in her voice, a nervousness that Evelyn hadn't detected before and she realised that she was in control of the situation now, she was the one with the authority and she was going to make damned sure she got what she wanted. She held up the poker again.

"Give me your name or I shall not let you leave." She used a firm, even tone; she wanted this girl to know that she meant what she said, she was not going to let her leave without the information she wanted. She had every right to demand to know the name of the thief that had stolen from her, regardless of whether they returned the items or not.

But the girl just smiled.

She smiled at Evelyn and then looked away quickly, as her cheeks blushed slightly.

"Then I should never speak again." The girl said the words in barely a whisper; Evelyn had to strain to hear and even then, she wasn't sure she had heard correctly. She looked at her, struggling to fathom what she was thinking, what thoughts were swimming behind those dark eyes, what hidden meaning was saturated within those words.

Evelyn knew the girl must be toying with her, manipulating her, delaying the inevitable with tricks and tactics. But then the thought struck her that maybe she wasn't, maybe she just wanted to stay, to stay there, in that room, in that moment, with Evelyn, for as long as possible. Maybe the girl didn't want to leave as much as

Evelyn didn't want her to go.

But she dismissed the thought, throwing it aside as quickly as it had entered her head. She would have no more ploys.

"Don't be daft," she said, as flippantly as she could muster. "I won't tell anyone." It was the only weapon she had left. It was the only thing she could think of to say to make sure the girl knew she was on her side. She just wanted to know, had to know, who she was. If she knew that then maybe she would know why she wanted her to stay.

"Bess," the girl said, quietly. "Call me Bess."

"Bess," repeated Evelyn, backing off and replacing the poker by the fire.

She had taken what she wanted from her. She had her name. She felt as though she owned a tiny part of her, possessed a small fraction of her. She would never have to give back that name. She could hold it, keep it, form the word with her lips, whisper it, think it. No one could take it away from her, and no one would know what it meant to her. It was a part of this girl that had now become hers.

She couldn't help but feel that they had formed a bond, that they had become closer, and she was surprised at the way it made her feel. She relaxed, and it felt warm and calm, as if the anger she'd felt at being kept in the dark had now dissipated and she could really start to find out who this girl was.

"I should go," said Bess, picking up her hat and coat.

"Wait!" said Evelyn, catching her arm as she reached for the window latch. Bess looked back.

Evelyn hadn't meant to sound so desperate, so panicked, but she couldn't help it, couldn't stop it. The word had come out before she was even aware she was saying it.

They stared at one another. Evelyn realised how mad she must look, how crazed, and, slowly, she released Bess' arm, fully aware that she was going to lose her, that she was letting this girl leave. But she couldn't understand why this mattered, why the girl meant so much. All Evelyn knew was she was losing a part of herself she'd only just discovered. And it hurt.

But they couldn't stay like that, held in that moment. They had to go their separate ways. But Evelyn wanted Bess to take a part of that moment with her, so she would know that Bess held a part of her, possessed something of her, always.

"Take this." She held out the locket.

Bess looked at it but shook her head.

"I can't take it. It's yours."

"Take it to remember me by." Evelyn held it out to her; she needed Bess to take it, she needed to know that the connection they'd formed would continue, that it wouldn't be severed the moment they parted.

"I don't need a locket to remember you."

Bess reached out and placed her hand firmly over Evelyn's. As their hands touched, she felt that same thrill of excitement rush through her that she had felt just moments before. But this time she didn't pull away. She couldn't pull away.

Bess leaned forward and gently kissed Evelyn. It was a brief, fleeting brush of lips. But it swelled Evelyn's chest, it filled her with a desire that she hadn't fully acknowledged, and when Bess pulled away, Evelyn reached out and pulled her back.

She reached her hand around Bess' neck and pulled her close. Their lips sank into one another; their kiss was deep and hungry. She wrapped her hand around Bess' back, holding her tight, refusing to let her go, as she felt the sweet taste of Bess' lips against her tongue. Bess' hands ran along her body—she wanted to sink into her, fall into her, be held and touched by her.

But then it was over. Bess pulled away.

"I have to go," she said, but she didn't look at Evelyn as she turned and opened the window. She was gone in an instant.

Evelyn stood, the cold rush of air from the window snapping her out of the heat of the moment. She couldn't quite believe what had happened, that she had just shared such an intimate moment with a girl, a girl she barely knew. She hadn't even believed that such a desire could exist, that such a passion could be inflamed within her and yet...

Then suddenly she doubted herself, doubted that it had happened, doubted it was real and not just a dream, a phantom in the dark. She rushed to the window and looked out in time to see a mounted figure riding into the darkness.

She knew that would be the last she saw of her, the last memory she would have of her. Perhaps that was best, perhaps it was right that it should end that way, to just become no more than a memory, a half-remembered dream, or a forgotten moment from her past that would be gone forever.

Slowly she closed the window and went to put the locket down, and then she noticed it, there on the side table, just as she had left it, the mask of the highwaywoman.

FOUR

The carriage charged along the road, rocking vigorously from side to side and shaking the passengers like toys in a box. Sunlight streamed in through the windows, heating up the already stifling air and suffocating everyone inside.

Evelyn slowly fanned herself, wafting warm and humid air towards her face in a vague attempt to cool her burning skin. She tugged on the laces of her bodice, trying to loosen their grip on her chest and give her room to breathe in the sweltering heat. But she was only half there, only half of her was on this nauseating journey; the other half was somewhere else—back in the room, back with the girl in the mask.

As she'd watched Bess leap from the window, she felt as though the highwaywoman was taking a part of her, wrenching it from her unwilling chest, and leaving her as

41

an empty shell. She hadn't realised how hollow she'd felt before that moment, how bare her life had seemed. Yet she still didn't understand why this girl had the effect of making her feel so alive.

She thought back to the woods, to how commanding Bess had been, as if she were a silent general presiding over the war of the roads. A warmth had shone through the veneer of strength: she had protected the child, protected her, and when all had seemed lost, Bess had appeared out of the dark to save her, as if summoned up by the shadows themselves.

Evelyn thought of her face, of the moment she had removed her mask and shown herself. She smiled as she remembered her beauty and her soft grace.

Briefly, unconsciously, her hand rose and touched her chest. Under her bodice, next to her bare skin, was the mask.

After she'd packed up her luggage, she'd seen it, lying on the side table. She looked at it for a moment, knowing she should leave it, knowing she should cast it aside and forget about the girl, forget about what had happened and just get home to move on with her life. But then she'd hurriedly thrust it into her bodice, and left the room to find a coach.

As she absently stroked the fabric of her dress she wondered if she would ever get the chance to see the girl again.

Suddenly the coach lurched backward and she was thrown from her seat. She dropped the fan and landed on her knees with a painful thud, as the people around her started calling out in confusion.

"What's happened?"

"Is everyone alright?"

'Not again!' she thought, hoisting herself back onto the seat, in the tiny, cramped space.

"I'll go and speak to the driver," one of the men was saying.

But Evelyn could hear shouting outside and before the man could reach for the door, it was wrenched open.

"Get out!" A masked woman stood at the foot of the steps, a pistol pointed into the carriage.

Evelyn's stomach twisted. It was Bess.

A flood of conflicting emotions hit her in a wave: she felt delight and joy at seeing her once more, seeing her beauty one more time, but she was angry that Bess was robbing coaches just hours after seeing her, after returning her money and locket. She had never considered that Bess had reformed, but she was still furious at the thought that Bess might steal from her all over again.

She sat, frozen, her eyes locked with the highwaywoman's, as one of the other passengers stood, dutifully, in an attempt to leave.

"Not you," Bess said. Her voice was low, almost a growl. "You." She gestured at Evelyn with the pistol.

'So, she does want the money back!' Evelyn thought angrily, enraged that the woman could be so disingenuous and inconsistent.

"I will not!" she shouted, boiling over with betrayal. "Are you raving mad?" The passengers stared at Evelyn in surprise, shocked that she could be so brave or foolish when a pistol was pointed directly toward her face.

"I do believe I am." Bess whispered the words, loud enough to hear, but whispered in the same way she'd whispered just before she'd given her name. Evelyn knew then, that it wasn't the money she'd come back for, it was her.

She couldn't go with her. It was madness, beyond madness, to go with her, to be with that woman, to alter her life, forever, to shed her world like an out of season gown.

She thought of her father, her horses, her duties, and the commitment she'd made. She thought of her house, her garden, the library, the loneliness, the boredom, the stifling and mundane world of social engagements, coffee mornings and afternoon tea. The same repetitive tasks stretched out before her, forcing her onto a path with no turns, no corners, no passion, no adventure, no love.

Bess reached out a hand, and Evelyn hesitated. She couldn't go.

But then the highwaywoman clicked the flintlock back on the pistol and Evelyn realised she didn't have a choice. The burden of responsibility had been lifted from her and she didn't have to concern herself with reasoning, she just had to allow herself to be taken.

She ignored the bemused faces of her fellow passengers as she reached out and took Bess' hand into her own. The moment their fingers touched, Evelyn felt a spark of excitement run through her and realised this moment had been inevitable since their eyes had first met.

Delicately, she picked her way past the passengers and down the carriage steps into the highwaywoman's waiting arms. She wanted to kiss her, to hold her and feel her soft lips beneath her own once more, but Bess pulled away and turned to the driver.

"As I said," she removed her hat and bowed theatrically, "I'm simply collecting a stray passenger."

The driver shook his head and giddied the horses into action, the wheels kicked up a cloud of dust as the carriage tumbled off down the road and Bess, still holding her hand tightly, led Evelyn towards a beautiful, chestnut mare grazing beside an oak tree.

The highwaywoman swung onto the horse with ease and reached down to Evelyn, who barely had time to wrap her arms around Bess before the horse took off at a gallop, back the way they had come.

Suddenly she remembered her trunk and all its contents, still strapped to the roof of the coach. She opened her mouth to shout to Bess, thinking of asking her to turn around and go back for it, but she stopped herself.

Everything that trunk contained was part of her old life, it would serve as a reminder, a solid, tangible memory of her past and of everything she had been. She didn't want to go back to that world, the world before she had met Bess. She felt as though she had been asleep her whole life and it was only now that she had woken up, she didn't want to go back into that misty, cloudy, empty, half-waking dream.

Now, the clothes on her back and the money in her purse were all that she owned and, for the first time in her life, she felt free.

Until her hand reached up to the chain hanging from her neck.

As Bess galloped onwards, Evelyn pulled the necklace from her bodice and clasped the small, golden locket in her hand.

The little golden heart she had been given, told to hold it close and let it act as a sign of her commitment to him.

***

"William Barrington, Esquire." He bowed to her and, as he did, he caught her eye and smiled.

She couldn't help but smile back—he was disarmingly charming, and she was so flustered with this sudden introduction that she was taken quite off-guard. He was a handsome young man: tall, but not too tall, and his features were smooth and attractive. She could see he had dark hair beneath his powdered wig and his smile was warm but roguish, and she felt there was more to this man than there first appeared. He gave the impression that he knew something she did not.

Then the thought struck her that perhaps it was her father's clumsy attempt to play matchmaker, anger flashed through her at the thought of the intrusion into her life. She glanced across at him to see if she could discern the intention behind this meeting, but her father simply grinned back and continued his introduction.

"Mr Barrington has been helping me with some matters of business, Evie my dear, and due to the lateness of the hour I have insisted he stay to dinner."

"The pleasure is mine," Mr Barrington said. His voice was deep and smooth; he spoke slowly and with purpose, and she felt he was summoning all his charm as he held her with a fixed gaze.

She wasn't in the mood to be charmed this evening, she had spent a dismal afternoon making light conversation with the young women in town and she was determined not to spend the evening in the same futile pursuit.

"What kind of business are you in, Mr Barrington?"

She decided that aloofness would allow her the opportunity to smile and nod without having to actually communicate.

"No, no, no, we'll have none of that! We've been talking business all afternoon!" Her father waved his hands emphatically and stepped between the couple, grabbing Mr Barrington, and leading him into the dining room. "Let us talk of Swift instead. Are you an admirer of the late Mr Swift, Barrington?"

She felt a mild sense of relief at having the conversation pulled from away from her so quickly, but she also felt slightly insulted that her choice of topic should be deemed so inappropriate.

"I am indeed, sir," replied Mr Barrington, "and I should be delighted to hear your opinion on his most controversial works." He shot Evelyn an apologetic look, as if regretful that their exchange should have ended so abruptly.

She felt a little sorry for him having to converse with her father, who had a tendency to talk at great length, and in great detail, on subject matters which others rarely shared equal passion for. But then she realised, with some relief, that matchmaking couldn't have been further from her father's mind and, at least on that count, she was spared.

The conversation continued over dinner—they drifted across literature, political affiliation, scientific endeavours, the exploration of Africa—and Evelyn received a proud pat on the hand from her father when he mentioned female novelists, as if she were a pioneer of the modern novel rather than simply a moderate fan.

She noticed that Mr Barrington allowed her father to

dominate the conversation. All through dinner, port, and cigars he continued his monologue while Mr Barrington listened attentively, occasionally glancing across at Evelyn who remained steadfastly silent.

She began to tire and kept looking at the clock, she had hoped to leave at the end of dinner, as would be appropriate when they had guests, however the opportunity had not presented itself and she was forced to stay long into the evening. She was flattered that her father had ignored etiquette on her behalf, but she was certain that it was simply to provide him with a larger audience for his opinion.

It wasn't until late into the night that she finally managed to slip out and retire to her room.

***

It was early the next morning, before breakfast, when she saw him again.

She hadn't expected him to still be at the house. However, it was likely that her father had not ended their dinner until the early hours, and so the offer of a bed for the night would be only natural.

She liked to see the garden in the morning, to see the mist rising from the ground and the plants covered with a delicate frost, giving the world around her a crystalline hue.

She had been following the little path through the wood, when she'd caught sight of a shadow up ahead. She'd stopped dead, tense and frightened. None of the servants had any cause to be outside, and the gardeners would not be about this early hour; her father would still be asleep. She crept ahead quietly, fearful that she had caught sight of a poacher, or a ghostly spirit.

But as she turned the corner and the trees cleared, she saw the familiar figure of Mr Barrington walking along the path up the house, stopping momentarily to admire the elm trees.

She hesitated, unsure if she should remain, or venture out and engage with her father's friend.

Politeness dictated she should act and so she started towards him.

"Mr Barrington!" she called, thinking it best to alert him to her presence rather than appear at his side without warning.

He turned to her and smiled as she came closer.

"Miss Thackeray," he said with a bow, "out for a morning stroll I see. I'm just on my way back toward the house. Would you care to join me?"

He held out his arm and she accepted it, looping her hand around his elbow. A silence descended upon them almost immediately. Evelyn had hoped that he would dominate the conversation, but she quickly saw that, as the hostess, she would have to lead.

"I hope my father didn't keep you awake all night with his lectures?"

"No, not at all," he laughed, a warm, slight laugh, without malice, "besides, I do find you father's opinion most… enlightening."

It was his hesitation that caught her ear, she wondered if he'd been as honest with her father about his preferences as it had seemed.

"Are you really an avid reader of Jonathan Swift, Mr Barrington?" she asked, feeling that she knew the answer already. Perhaps the mutual tedium of the previous night's conversation was now a shared secret. She couldn't help but smile at the thought of how patient a man Mr Barrington must be, to endure the lectures of her father longer than even his own daughter had managed.

"To be honest with you, Miss Thackeray, I'm much more of a Fielding man"

"Sarah Fielding?" she gasped with delight. "OH, I adore her! I read all her books as a girl and you know she doesn't live too far from here, in Bath as a matter of fact, I thought perhaps that I might go and see her but as yet I haven't been able to gain an invitation—"

"Actually, I was referring to Mr Henry Fielding."

"Oh… of course you were!" She felt her face turn hot at the shame of assuming a man such as Mr William Barrington would read works composed by a woman and intended for children, she knew she must have insulted him, and immediately tried to take back her thoughtless words. "I'm sorry, it was foolish of me to think that you would be reading Sarah Fielding…" Evelyn tried not to catch his eye, unwilling to see the reaction of a man who was either angry with her or laughing at her.

"No, not at all, in fact I've heard that her work is quite admirable, I simply prefer a story that will make me laugh."

She did look up at him then; there was no trace of contempt or mockery in his eyes and she relaxed under his gaze. For the first-time Evelyn started to feel as if she could warm to Mr Barrington, as if she could let down her guard a little in his presence.

"Well from what I've heard," she teased, "he relies purely on bawdiness to entertain. I think I'll stick to Sarah."

He laughed out loud, and Evelyn was delighted that

she'd made a joke he'd liked and thought that perhaps there was hope of a friendship between them.

"I should think you are probably right to," he said.

They talked further as they continued up to the house, but it was disappointing when they reached the front door and, rather than coming inside to join her for breakfast and continue the conversation, Mr Barrington made his excuses and left. He bowed once again and promised that they would talk further in the future, before disappearing off to the stables to fetch his horse.

She smiled to herself thinking back over their brief talk, and there was a lightness to her gait as she wandered into the house to sit down to breakfast with her father.

It wasn't until later in the day that Evelyn realised how much she missed William Barrington, how much she missed having someone her own age, with her own interests, to talk to. Sitting alone in her large, empty library, and looking out over the large, empty garden, Evelyn hoped it wouldn't be the last time she saw Mr Barrington.

***

Over the next few weeks William Barrington appeared to make excuses to visit the house rather more often than she believed to be strictly necessary.

It was less than a week after their first walk together that he was back in the house and staying for dinner, only this time her father didn't dominate the conversation. Slowly, Evelyn started to come out of the shell she had built around herself, no longer holding back on her opinion and each time she made a joke she glanced across to Mr Barrington to check on the effect it had.

Each time he visited they would always find the opportunity to stroll in the garden together, despite the winter cold. Their conversation grew more varied and animated over the following weeks and Evelyn felt more contented, relieved that there were other people like her, with the same thoughts and opinions and intelligence. She decided that if there was one Mr Barrington, then there would be others and she may well be able to find a place for herself in the world, where she could finally be happy.

It was a still and wintry morning when, once again, they were walking up the tree-lined path towards the house. The bare branches were sprinkled with a light frost and the only sounds were their feet crunching through the gravel, and the occasional, isolated cawing of a crow.

The conversation had lulled into silence, but Evelyn felt comfortable enough in Mr Barrington's company that she thought little of it.

"Miss Thackeray?" he said suddenly.

"Yes?" She waited for him to continue but he seemed to struggle. "Are you quite alright, Mr Barrington?"

"It's your father, or, I mean… well, I have spoken to your father…"

"At great length and on many occasions…" said Evelyn, trying to fathom what point he was making.

"No, I mean yes, of course, only…" He took a breath. "I have spoken to your father about you, with regards to your future—"

"My future?"

"Our future."

"Our future?"

"All of our futures, yours, mine, your father's. It affects us all."

"What affects us all?" She stopped and turned to him, worried. "Mr Barrington, what affects us all?"

He stared back at her for a moment and then dropped to his knee on the ice-covered ground.

"I have come to look upon you with great admiration and respect." He clasped her hand and, whilst Evelyn was surprised, she said nothing. "You have shown yourself to be a most admirable and unselfish young woman and I would be most honoured, most honoured, if you would consent to be my wife."

Niamh Murphy

FIVE

She was silent for a long time before eventually managing to stutter, "I-I don't know what to say, I…"

He stood and bowed, no longer looking at her.

"Please accept my sincerest apologies, Miss Thackeray. I can see that I have greatly embarrassed you." He was formal, a glass wall had descended across him and his jovial self had disappeared completely. "But I beg of you, do not reject me outright. Take some time to think it over. I am going into town on business and shall be back in a few days. Please think of me well."

With that he turned and left.

Evelyn was stunned and stood staring into space for some time before she realised the cold.

She walked back up to the house. Her mind was racing; there were so many thoughts flashing in and out, that she had trouble catching them and making sense of what had just occurred.

She wondered if she should have known this was about to happen, if there had been some sign, some warning of his intent. Thinking back, she could pin nothing down—she had been cordial to him, friendly, but no more so than she would be with any other friend.

But now she was in a dilemma, he had forced her into a position where she would have to provide an answer, she would have to reject him and by doing so she would lose the only friend that she had.

Or perhaps she shouldn't reject him.

Since they had met, she had thought of Mr Barrington as a friend, a charming and engaging friend. She could talk to him about her interests and enjoyed his company and his wit. She had not, for a moment, considered marriage. But perhaps she had been naïve, perhaps she should have seen his intentions, perhaps she had not made her own intentions clear. By spending time alone with a young unmarried man, perhaps it had been her that had been giving the signals towards marriage—after all, what young woman of her age is not contemplating marriage?

Perhaps she should be considering marriage. If all women her age were considering marriage then there was good reason for them to do so. Happiness, security, a family, status—the voice of a wife is louder than the voice of a maid.

She was a fool not to have seen this coming. A fool not to have known he would have been thinking of it. But there it was; the offer had been made. Only she didn't know what to think of it. Would she be happier married?

She thought about writing to her old friend, Mary.

They had grown up together in Cambridge and had shared so much, but when Mary had married their friendship had faded. But now she could write to her, ask her advice, her opinion: her experience in marriage would help her decide. But a reply may take days, perhaps even weeks, and even then, she doubted she could convey the true extent of her feelings in writing.

Evelyn wondered how she could determine future happiness. She certainly liked Mr Barrington, but she wasn't convinced that a few conversations around the garden were enough to gauge the possibility of a good marriage. But then what was?

Perhaps friendship was enough; a good friendship, with a good man. That was so much more than many women had at the start of a marriage.

She thought of her parents. They'd had a long and happy marriage. They'd shared twenty years of contentment and security. She thought back to their time together—she'd witnessed barely a cross word between them, they talked together for long hours, always content in one another's company. Evelyn knew they'd wanted more children, but even so the house had been filled with laughter and joy. It was a marriage she wanted for herself, but she didn't know how to obtain it, how to ensure that kind of love within marriage.

She decided to consult her father. Perhaps he would know, perhaps he would be able to tell her how she could turn friendship into love, or whether it was even possible. More determined, with a goal in mind, Evelyn almost ran the last few steps up to the house. She removed her cloak and went straight into his study where she knew he would always be at this hour.

He was sitting quietly in a large armchair, pulled up to the fire, immersed in a book.

"Did you love mother?" she demanded. He looked up, startled.

"Of course, I did!"

"From the beginning?"

"From the moment I saw your mother, I knew I would marry her. She was walking in the garden, one very much like the garden here at Abberton, as a matter of fact. It was June I believe; her parents had been invited by my uncle—"

He continued his narrative and Evelyn half listened as she remembered her mother, who had been so happy and so warm. But then those last few months...

It had been so hard to see her fade, to see her grow thinner, more haggard. Her face, which had been so full of life, misted over as she grew weak. Her smile became rarer, her waking hours, fewer. She withdrew from society, then from the garden, and the house, until she was an invalid, never leaving her room.

But as hard as it had been to see her fade, it had been harder once she'd gone.

Her death cast a dark shadow over the house and her father had fallen into a deep, unshakable despair. It had taken months before he had been able to leave his room. Evelyn had nursed him through his grief, but in doing so she'd had to hide her own.

She had grown distant from her friends. As they had excitedly chased young men across ballrooms, she had stood back and watched with apathy. It all seemed so fruitless and uninteresting. She no longer cared for the latest gossip or fashion and when young gentlemen asked her to dance, she politely declined, to the horror of her peers.

It was a visit from her Aunt and Uncle that finally shook the last of the grief from her father. They had arrived one afternoon without warning, simply pulling up in their carriage and announcing that they were staying indefinitely. Her father's sister, Margaret, and her husband, Mr Jacob Haverhill, were determined to see the household change its spirits. It had been a joy to have them there, but at first Evelyn did not believe them to be capable of bringing her father out of his melancholic state. She feared that he would simply slide away in grief.

But on the third day of their visit, her Aunt Margaret refused to leave her father's rooms. A deathly silence descended over the house, while Evelyn could only wonder what was happening. In the afternoon she heard shouting, she'd never heard her father so enraged, and her uncle disappeared into the rooms as well, leaving Evelyn to pace the floor of the drawing room alone.

She never discovered what conversation had taken place between them all, but from her father's later actions, she started to guess.

By the end of her aunt and uncle's stay, Evelyn's father was a changed man. He ate, he talked, he even laughed again and Evelyn had become the centre of his world. He seemed to live for her and she realised that they must have convinced him that although he had lost a wife, he still had a daughter.

Not only did she have new gowns, jewellery, and books but he lavished his time upon her as well. They would talk long into the evening, he encouraged her to read more widely and they would enter into lengthy discussions on novels and politics, history, liberty and even the latest science.

She started to feel whole again, that the weight of her father's grief had been lifted from her shoulders and she was freer to live her life, but she still wasn't happy. She had become bored with Cambridge, with its endless cycle of social events, and her silly friends, whose interests and pursuits seemed so vacuous once she began to see how brief and transient life can be.

Once she mentioned this to her father, he too admitted that he felt as though the town, the house and the memories of their old life were getting too much for him to bear and so he put all his effort into finding them a new home.

He decided that they would move to Bristol.

He found a suitable estate with a large and charming Tudor manor, although some of it had started to fall into disrepair. There were large gardens, stables, and its proximity to both the booming port of Bristol and the literary town of Bath meant that Mr Thackeray could invest his time in discovering new business ventures whilst Evelyn could find a new selection of intellectual peers with whom she could socialise.

Although it had been sad at first to leave behind a home with so many memories, it was also refreshing to enter a new place, a new world. The bustling port was brimming with activity and life from every corner of the globe; it was constantly moving and changing with the tides and was a world that Mr Thackeray found exhilarating. In the other direction was Bath, an ancient and beautiful town and through various introductions Evelyn opened herself up to a new crowd of writers, poets, intellectuals and academics and she felt as if there was so much promise and hope in her new life.

But the novelty did not stay with her for long.

As her father spent more and more time away from home, conducting meetings and discussing trade, Evelyn began to get bored with their new life.

She started to see, in Bristol and Bath, the same repeating patterns of life as she had seen in Cambridge. The seasons and the locations had changed, but the same faces danced the same dances and spread the same inane gossip and pursued the same pointless pursuits.

Gradually Evelyn stopped going to the balls and the dances and the coffee mornings and the afternoon teas. More and more she withdrew to her gardens and her precious library.

"Did you want something, Evie?" His sudden question startled her out of her trance.

"Oh, I don't know." She pulled a book from one of the shelves and began flicking through its pages absent-mindedly. Her father waited patiently for her to continue.

"It's Mr Barrington," she said finally.

"Ah, Mr Barrington. I see. He is a charming young man, don't you think?"

"Yes, he is."

"And very good with the dogs."

"Is he?"

"Well, something Garret said, I'm sure it was about the dogs, or maybe the horses—"

"He asked me to marry him."

"Garret?"

"No, not Garret, Mr Barrington. Just now in the garden."

"And what did you say?"

"Aren't you surprised?"

"Not in the least! He asked my permission."

"Oh, yes of course, I suppose he must have done."

"So, what did you say, Evelyn?" Mr Thackeray peered at his daughter. She'd started flicking through pages again.

"He told me to give him my answer when I'm ready."

"Well that was decent of him, wasn't it?"

"What do you think of him, Father?"

"Oh, well I've never been a good judge of character," he said. "I left that sort of thing to your mother, but he does appear to be an amiable sort of fellow."

"So, you do like him?"

"I do indeed. He has some interesting business ideas and seems more than willing to take on the running of this place—"

"You talked about the estate?"

"Of course, we did, my dear! I could never give my approval to someone who'd... oh, I don't know, run off to the colonies with you and start a plantation. No, we discussed everything in great depth. He's agreed to invest a great deal of money and of course in return he would take over the house and lands upon my... retirement."

"So, we wouldn't be able to leave Abberton?" She didn't know why, but the thought of staying in the same house made her feel trapped.

"Should you wish to stay, everything has been arranged. However, should you wish to go back to Cambridge, of course, that would not be impossible." He smiled reassuringly at her as she sat on the chaise longue, her book resting open on her knee.

William Barrington was a like-minded spirit. He was

kind, and gentle. He talked to her about what she was interested in and listened to her opinion in a way that few other people did, he never belittled her or patronised her and he regarded her with respect and admiration. He would be a good match.

But she did not love him.

She wondered if there was any point in marriage if there was no love, if there was any point in anything if there was no love.

But then she remembered her mother, and the broken man her father had become when he'd lost her. Evelyn began to realise that if she never fell in love then she would never have to feel the kind of searing anguish she had to witness her father endure.

Evelyn looked at her father. He was turning into an old man, his stomach was growing, his hair was thinning, and his bright eyes were looking out at her from a tired face. He needed someone to take care of the estate when he no longer could; she knew, from occasional unsubtle hints, that he wanted to see grandchildren before he was too old to appreciate them, he would need security and he would want to know that she was being cared for after he was gone.

She sighed as she admitted there was no good reason not to accept.

"I suppose that's settled then," she said.

***

The garden was always at its best in summer; although her favourite flowers, the bright red witch-hazel, blossomed in the winter months, it was hard not to be taken in by the lush wave of colour brought about by the early heat of June.

Evelyn knew this was the last time she would see the garden for a while; everything around her was starting to change and, even though she had acknowledged it was going to have to, she still wanted to hold on to her old life as it was, for just one more walk. Although she had accepted the offer in words, her heart was still reluctant.

Luckily, Mr Barrington hadn't been as eager to get married as he had been to become engaged and she felt that she had been granted a temporary reprieve, time to become used to the idea, to plan her future and find her way to becoming happy.

It had been six months since the proposal, and in that time Mr Barrington had been forced to spend weeks at a time away on business. He explained that he needed to make preparations and ensure that everything would be in place for them to have a secure foundation for marriage. But with each passing week, fresh doubts had started to spring up in Evelyn's mind.

When he had suggested that she travel to Cambridge to visit her old friend, she realised he must have sensed her discomfort, and part of her thanked him for that. She would stay with Mary, and see a new marriage at first hand, perhaps take advice and secure within herself the frame of mind she would need for her new way of life.

Slowly, she walked back up to the house and towards the carriage that awaited her. She was already packed and dressed for travel and she could see her father was hurrying the servants along while Mr Barrington stood by, patiently watching events.

There wasn't much time left.

Her father had initially demanded she make use of the family carriage and take several of the servants, including her lady's maid, with her to Cambridge. But she had refused. If she was going to be able to think while she was away, to clear her mind and allow herself to get used to the idea of becoming a married woman, then she needed to be free from everything that reminded her of home—every servant, every carriage, everything that affected her independence.

Mr Thackeray had thought she was mad, and there was a moment when she thought they may actually enter into an argument on the matter.

But then Mr Barrington had stepped in, calmly and respectfully coming between father and daughter during an afternoon tea. To her eternal gratitude, he had defended her position, insisting that it was to Cambridge, not the heart of Africa, that she travelled and, once there, she would be able to avail herself of her good friend's servants without impediment.

Reluctantly Mr Thackeray had agreed, but not without insisting he supervised all the travel arrangements personally. Evelyn was greatly relieved and reassured in Mr Barrington's affections for her, feeling that perhaps things did bode well for a comfortable marriage after all.

"Evelyn! There you are; everything is ready. Do you wish to take a book with you for the journey?" Her father fussed and clucked over her like a broody chicken.

She shook her head: the thought of reading, whilst rocking and shaking along the track into town, made her feel queasy.

"Is everything ready?" she asked, already knowing the answer.

"Yes! Yes! Everything is packed and ready for you—you're going to stop at The Swan in town, and then catch the stagecoach to—"

"I know Father, I know. I have the journey all written down." She pulled the instructions from her pocket and waved them at him, but as she did she saw the sadness in his eyes and she felt her resolve waver. She stepped forward, taking him into an embrace. "I shall miss you," she whispered.

Although it was only a few weeks, it would be the longest they had ever spent apart and she knew that when she came back, nothing would be the same again: she would no longer be his daughter, she would be Mr Barrington's wife, and she realised it wasn't just her that was struggling to accept the change.

She pulled back and smiled at her father before catching Mr Barrington's eye.

He looked a little tired and drawn; it seemed that the preparations for the marriage were starting to weigh a little heavily on him. But when he smiled at her, his whole manner changed. He was dashing and childish, and had been so good to her; she knew she was being unfair to him with her reluctance and hoped that perhaps one day she would be able to somehow make up for that.

"I have something for you, Evelyn," he said, pulling a small box from within his coat pocket.

She still hadn't become used to him using her Christian name, but knew it was his attempt to cultivate affection between them and so had allowed him to continue. However, she had yet to return the favour.

He held the little box out to her and, tentatively, she took it from him, wondering if it might contain a thimble or a ring as a sign of engagement. She was a little surprised to find it held a necklace.

It was a small, golden, heart-shaped pendant, and, as she pulled it from the box, she saw that it had a little catch in the side. Glancing back at Mr Barrington for reassurance, she opened it to read the engraving inside:

To My Darling Evelyn
Yours Always
WB

"It's for you to wear over your heart, while you're away from me," he said.

She stared at it; although it wasn't a ring, it was as just as good as one. It was a clear symbol of their agreement, of his affection and her commitment.

"Thank you," she said. "I don't know what to say."

She placed the locket around her neck and stalled for a moment, unsure if she should embrace him, instead she held out her hand and he bowed and kissed it.

'All will be well,' she told herself, forcing the sincerest smile she could muster.

Evelyn said goodbye again and then ascended the steps into the carriage; as soon as she took her seat, the horses started and the carriage pulled away. She leaned out the little window; her father and Mr Barrington stood on the steps of Abberton Hall, growing smaller as she lurched forward. She waved to them, and then the carriage turned the corner at the end of the driveway and they disappeared, along with the house, its contents, its people, and the sheltered, quiet life she had known.

As soon as it was gone she wanted it back.

Niamh Murphy

SIX

"STOP!"

Bess jumped at the sudden shout and the horse buckled.

"Stop, please! You must stop!"

Bess brought the horse to a standstill on the muddy track.

"What is it?" she turned to Evelyn, concerned.

"We must turn back!" Her voice was filled with alarm.

"I don't understand. If you're worried about your trunk we can—"

"No! NO! I have to get back to the coach!" She knew she had to go back, she knew that she had made the wrong choice.

"What's wrong?" Bess asked, slowly and with composure.

"I can't do this!" Evelyn was frantic—she could feel the panic rising in her chest, she gripped the highwaywoman's waist tightly and her breath was coming in rapid bursts. She needed to get off the horse, to go back; she'd walk if she had to.

"Let's just stop here for a while." Bess said, slipping off the horse and turning to help Evelyn to the ground.

She almost leapt off and fell into Bess' arms, clinging to her like a wildcat, taking in gulps of air. She was so angry with herself for running, for betraying her father and Mr Barrington, they had both been so good to her, so kind, they had done everything within their power to help her, and she had returned the favour by running off.

"Shh, shh, shh, shh." Bess softly stroked her hair and then kissed her head slowly. "It's alright" she whispered.

"I don't know what I'm doing!" Evelyn said finally. "I can't believe I just ran away!" Her breathing was slower but, as she thought of her father, she felt her chest tighten. "I can't do this." She pulled out of the embrace and looked up at Bess. "I shouldn't have done this," she said, defeated by her responsibilities.

"You wanted to come with me, I know you did, I felt it last night when—"

"I know." Evelyn looked back down the road, the carriage had long gone but it was as if she could still see it in the distance, getting further away. "I know. It's just... I'm giving up so much and I don't know what I'm doing it for." She looked back at Bess again. "I'm so sorry."

Bess smiled painfully.

"It's alright," she said, "you can go back. Of course, you can go back." She reached up and pulled the mask from her face. Evelyn had almost forgotten how beautiful she was. "All I ask is that you spend the day with me. Spend a few hours with me and then I will take you back. We can ride over to Ashford and you can catch another carriage from there."

"But what about money? And my things?"

"I'll pay for the carriage, and they will probably unload your trunk at the inn in Bristol and leave it there for you to collect." Her voice was calm, measured, reasonable, and everything she said made sense.

Evelyn breathed out slowly, trying to think; her father would be worried when she didn't arrive, but she was already a day late so a few extra hours wouldn't matter, she would explain that she had been robbed which had caused the delay and her things had been stolen. No one would ever know, no one need ever find out about her minor indiscretion, her moment of weakness, about the woman she had been willing to give up her way of life for. She could slip back into her routine unnoticed.

She had time. She had time to spend the rest of the day with Bess, to enjoy freedom without consequence, to live how she wished to live for a few small hours. She smiled at the thought and felt the panic fall away.

"Alright," she said, "I'll spend the day with you."

Bess smiled and nodded, accepting the decision with grace. She held out her hand and Evelyn took it eagerly, allowing herself to be guided along by the highwaywoman.

The road stretched ahead of them just a few yards, before disappearing out of sight around a field boundary. A soft heat haze had settled, giving everything an ethereal glow, and Evelyn felt as though she were travelling along a path to another world.

Tall, lush green hedges lined the track, broken by the

occasional tree, and blackberries hung like dew drops all along the brambles. Evelyn allowed her hand to drift through the tall grasses at the side of the road, enjoying the sensation as they tickled her fingers. Dragonflies hummed around the bushes, hovering momentarily before darting off, grasshoppers filled the warm air with their lazy summer song and the occasional wood pigeon and starling chipped in with their own leisurely contribution, all chiming in with the soft clipping of the horse's hooves against the hard dirt track.

Golden fields peeked through gaps here and there along the hedge and the smell of freshly cut hay wafted on the breeze. Evelyn could hear the shouts of several farm workers and a dog's barks carried on the warm air. She closed her eyes, letting herself relax and enjoy the few short hours of freedom she had.

"I used to ride along here as a child," Bess said suddenly.

"I can imagine that," said Evelyn, smiling at the thought of a young Bess, her hair loose and flowing behind her, as she galloped along the country roads. "I see you as wild and rebellious!"

"No actually, I always did as I was told." There was a note of sadness in her voice and she turned to Evelyn. "How about you?"

"Oh, I was a terrible child! My mother used to despair!" she laughed. "She always used to say, 'I don't know what will become of you, young lady' and then she would try to teach me the etiquette of something or other. She threatened to send me to a finishing school at one point but my father was having none of it. I think that was the only time I ever knew them to argue…" Evelyn trailed off as she remembered those last few years, remembering how her mother became weaker and her father watched the centre of his world wither away." 'My light.'"

"Sorry?"

"That's what he called her; his 'light'. She was his guiding light and then when she was gone… he was lost … directionless…"

"He has you though, hasn't he?"

"Yes, he does." Evelyn stopped and looked to Bess. "That's why I have to go back. You do understand, don't you?"

"Yes. Yes, I do." Bess reached up to stroke her face. "I promise I will get you back to him. No matter what else happens you will get back to him safely, alright?"

Evelyn smiled and nodded.

"We are supposed to be enjoying our time together!" she said wondering how the mood had become so sombre. "How shall we spend the day?"

Bess still seemed tense and Evelyn hoped that she hadn't ruined the little time they had left.

"Ah, well," Bess looked down the road, "we could start to make our way slowly over to Ashford… I know a beautiful glen where we could stop on the way."

Suddenly this fearsome bandit seemed sheepish and Evelyn smiled, trying to imagine the reasons behind Bess wanting to stop in a 'beautiful glen'.

"That sounds lovely," she said and Bess, once again, took her by the hand and led her along the track.

The road was gradually getting steeper and Evelyn was becoming more and more aware of the heat pressing down on her as she struggled to climb. Her shoes were not meant for walking any great distance and they had begun to rub against her heels, causing painful blisters. Bess, on the other hand, was untroubled by the hike and seemed determined to reach the top as quickly as possible, pulling Evelyn along behind her.

"Would you like to go back on the horse?" she asked, glancing back.

Evelyn thought of the chafing and her twisted spine.

"No, I'm fine," she said, hoping that they would reach the top of the hill soon, and stop.

As they reached the crest, Evelyn could see fields spread out before her, a great ocean of gold. In the distance, she could make out a few people harvesting, tearing the corn up with scythes and leaving bunches, standing to dry, all around the field like great corn dollies. Not far from them was a little hamlet with a few houses and a water mill.

Suddenly she felt a pang of jealousy. They had such simple lives: they wouldn't have great social commitments, there would be no need for etiquette and no pressures of running an estate, they could freely choose who they wanted to marry, they didn't have to worry about commitments and inheritance, all they had to think about was finishing a good day's work.

"I'm so glad I'm not breaking my back in those fields," said Bess, and then pointed down the hill to a little wood. "That's where we're going, that little glen over there," she said. "It really is incredible."

Evelyn looked at Bess as she stared across the valley. She was beautiful—her features soft, her eyes dark; she seemed troubled and distracted and Evelyn felt a surge of regret at leaving her. But she knew she couldn't stay, knew that they couldn't run around the countryside forever. She had to go home.

The heat was wearing her down and she was beginning to get rather thirsty. She wanted to hide in the shade and, mercifully, the road sloped downhill so she could start to enjoy her summer's day as they made their way towards the wood at a leisurely stroll.

The road levelled out and joined up with a small stream, which babbled happily alongside them and, as they drew closer to the trees, Evelyn could hear birdsong, a cacophony of different melodies all vying to be the loudest and most beautiful.

They came to the edge of the wood and Bess led Evelyn into the trees, stopping just beyond the tree line, and it was a blessed relief for her to finally be out of the hot sun. Bess turned to her, still holding her hand; she brushed back a lock of Evelyn's hair that had fallen loose and sighed heavily.

"Whatever happens," Bess' voice was barely above a whisper, "I need you to know that what happened between us was real."

There was a look of concern intermingled with fear on the highwaywoman's face. Evelyn smiled reassuringly.

"I know," she said softly.

She reached up to touch Bess' face and stroked the soft skin of her cheek, wondering if she really would be able to walk away from this girl at the end of the day. She wasn't sure she could just walk back into the life she had known before meeting her, if she could just be as she was before. Suddenly she dreaded the moment they would part, the thought of never seeing her again and of trying to shut down the feelings that had been awakened inside of her.

"Come back with me." The words were out before she

realised.

Bess sighed and drew Evelyn closer.

"I can't," she whispered. "Not yet." Bess pulled out of the embrace and gave Evelyn a half smile. "I have to show you something."

She took hold of Evelyn's hand and led her deeper into the wood.

The brook was running through the trees and they followed a well-trodden path towards a little clearing. Here the stream flowed into a large clear pool, the sun pierced through the trees and glittered across the surface, a lonely willow draped its leaves into the water and a kingfisher stood on a branch, proudly surveying his realm.

"It's beautiful." Evelyn said turning to Bess and smiling.

But the highwaywoman didn't smile back.

"I'm so sorry," she said.

Evelyn was puzzled for a moment. Then she caught Bess glance at something to her left. Evelyn followed her gaze and gasped. There, in the lonely glen, tall, bearded and masked, was a highwayman.

"You're late," he said.

The last thing Evelyn saw before she fell was the back end of a musket.

SEVEN

Her head was pounding and her joints were stiff. She tried to take a deep breath and stop the sickness rising in her stomach but the stench of wood smoke and strong alcohol filled her lungs and made her wheeze.

Her skin was painfully hot along one side of her body, she could hear the sharp crackling of a fire to her left and to her right there was shouting. Indistinct voices, she tried to concentrate and pick out words. Then she heard Bess, loud above the others.

"No!" She was shouting, her voice shrill, more panic than anger. "You can't!"

"And what are you going to do about it?" said another voice, a deep guttural growl—the voice from the glen.

Evelyn forced her eyes open, but it was hazy and too

bright. She closed them again, pacing herself. The voices were rising; Bess was standing her ground, but there were other voices, also men, also angry, and she was sure she recognised them from before. Evelyn forced herself to look, forced herself, with all her might, to open her eyes.

She was next to a fireplace, a huge stone hearth with a roaring fire blazing inside. As she looked round, searching for Bess, she could see she was in a kitchen, an old kitchen with a large wooden table, but little else; it was bare. There was no food, all the pots and pans were gone and the windows had their shutters tightly closed.

As her eyes adjusted she could make out a huge figure towering above a woman, Bess, she had her back to Evelyn and was shouting at the man, suddenly he struck her hard with the back of his hand. She stumbled and fell to the ground.

Evelyn gasped as the tall highwayman strode out of the dark towards her. She tried to get up, tried to move, but she was stuck fast; her hands bound to the arms of a chair.

She wanted to scream but only a rasping cry came out.

He laughed as he stared down at her. The flickering, orange glow of the hot fire made him more terrifying, as he leaned into her. He no longer wore his mask and above his thick black beard she could see his pockmarked skin and black eyes in all their repulsive glory. She tried to squirm away as he stroked her face, his rough skin reeking of tobacco and, when he spoke, his breath was heavy with gin and foetid meat.

"You be a good girl for Johnny now," he whispered, reaching into his belt he pulled out a knife and went to slice through her bodice.

"Get off her!" Bess was at his side, her sword to his

cheek. Blood dripped from her lip and Evelyn felt relief that, once again, Bess was stepping in to save her.

"What 'ave I told you?" Johnny asked, standing to his full height, and glaring down at the highwaywoman, who seemed frail and tiny in comparison.

"And what have I told you?" she replied, holding her rapier steady as she pulled a pistol from her belt and clicked back the flintlock.

He started to laugh, a loud booming laugh that shook the room and grated on Evelyn's bones. Suddenly someone else appeared out of the darkness to stand at Bess' side. Evelyn had seen him before, laughing while robbing the coach. He wasn't laughing now.

"Johnny, just leave it," he said quietly. He sounded exasperated.

Johnny eyed him with suspicion.

"Charlie, you little dog! Always trying to be a gentleman, ain't you! Well a title and good talkin' are worth nothing in the world, are they Bessie?"

"Alright lads, come on!" barked yet another voice, buried in the darkness, out of Evelyn's sight. "We're late as it is; there'll be plenty more skirt down the pub, Johnny."

It had an effect: Johnny lowered his knife and leaned forward to Bess.

"You're lucky," he whispered, before moving off.

The kitchen door opened; Evelyn had expected it to be dark outside but sunshine streamed in from the courtyard and two men walked out into the light. She realised it couldn't be more than a couple of hours since she'd been walking in the glen. The highwayman, Charlie, glanced at Bess.

"Will you be alright?" he asked. She nodded and he

patted her shoulder before following the others out and closing the kitchen door.

Bess breathed out slowly and replaced the pistol and sword in her belt.

"I'm sorry," she whispered as she knelt to untie Evelyn.

"What happened?" As her hand was loosened Evelyn reached up to touch her head, it was pounding and stung where she touched it, she could feel a large lump forming under a gash. "The last thing I remember is the woods and that man…" She trailed off, starting to feel light-headed at the memory.

"You were knocked out," Bess said, loosening the last of the ropes, "and brought here."

"Well we must escape!" But she caught the look on Bess' face, a look filled with guilt and shame. "I've seen those men before," said Evelyn slowly, "I saw them with you during the robbery…"

She allowed her accusation to hang in the air.

"It's not what it looks like."

"So, you didn't know that… that beast would be waiting for us?"

Bess looked away.

"I don't understand," continued Evelyn, "you said you could see why I had to go back, you promised you would get me back to my father, we were going to go to Ashford and… and…" Evelyn felt her voice start to break and stopped.

"I did promise" said Bess, "and I will keep to that promise, I will get you home… I just need a bit of time."

"Time? What for? Take me home! Get me on a carriage…." she breathed heavily, she felt too weary to fight. "What do you want of me?" she asked quietly.

She was tired, sick and confused. She had been stupid in leaving the carriage, stupid in thinking she could run off into the wilderness with a thief and expect everything to be wonderful. Bess took her by the arms and looked up at her.

"They want a ransom for you—"

"They?"

"The others, they want a ransom for you and your father will pay. He'll pay, I'll get you home and everything will be alright." She looked at Evelyn with such sincerity that it felt almost acceptable.

"And you would do as they ask?"

"I have to, Evelyn! I have to, or they'll kill me. They won't kill you, you're too precious, but they will take me out to the nearest tree and hang me without a second thought." Her eyes were desperate, a bruise had started to form on her cheek and the blood from her mouth had dripped on to her shirt.

"But… just now you seemed to manage…"

"I can fend them off," she said. "I can only just fend them off but I cannot go against them, there is too much at stake."

"So, what do you want?" Evelyn asked finally.

"What?"

"What do you want with me?"

"I…"

"I mean, everything you said, everything you did, it was all just to get me here, wasn't it?" She was angry at Bess and angry at herself for being taken in.

"No!"

"Everything you've said to me has just been to stop yourself from getting hurt!"

81

"Hanged!" Bess corrected. "And no, I tried to get you away; I didn't want them to get to you. They were going to take you from the inn where you were staying, but I made sure you got a carriage in the morning, I wanted you to get out of London—"

"And then you came and got me anyway, it was you at the carriage, with a pistol, you that led me to the woods—"

"Would you have preferred Johnny? He would have broken your legs!"

"Well at least he wouldn't have broken my heart!" It was out before she could stop it, out before she even knew she had meant it.

She looked away from her, humiliated. She felt stupid for following her, stupid for believing her and being betrayed by her. She steadied her jaw and tried to breathe; she could feel a sob rising in her throat and pushed it back down, buried it before it could be exposed.

"I can't help what's happened." Bess spoke quietly, her voice was close to Evelyn's ear but Evelyn refused to turn and look at her, she kept her eyes focused on the flames in the hearth. "And I can't change things. We must see this through but I promise that I will look after you and I will make sure that you get back to your father safely. I meant all of those things Evelyn, I meant them..."

Evelyn felt Bess stroke the back of her hand and she turned to look at her. She had such deep dark eyes; they seemed so earnest, so beautiful. Evelyn desperately wanted to trust her, wanted her to be telling the truth and to help her. She felt her pride getting in the way, resisting the urge to accept her help but common sense reminded her she had no one else to trust. She sighed.

"Alright," she said reluctantly, "but how can you keep

me safe?"

"I have a key for one of the upstairs rooms; you'll be safe in there."

Evelyn nodded. She was slightly unsteady on her feet, and Bess helped her navigate the narrow wooden stairs out of the kitchen and into the main house.

The corridors were small and dark, there was precious little light and everywhere smelt musty and damp. Bess took her through a door and out into the entrance hall. Bright daylight broke through cracks in the boards on the windows and dust danced in the sunbeams. She could see that the hall had been quite impressive at one point—it was spacious with bright wallpaper, but now it was dark and grubby, the floor was covered in sheets and there were oddly shaped shadows scattered everywhere. She hoped it was just covered furniture, but the effect was eerie and unsettling. She gripped Bess' arm, suddenly imagining the shapes moving towards them, closing in on them.

Bess led her up the grand oak staircase onto the first floor; everything was strange and misshapen. It felt oddly quiet as if the whole house was resting, waiting for something, watching her move around its sanctuary, violating its quiet rest. She didn't like the house. She didn't like the darkness and the shadows and the hidden recesses, she didn't know how many more highwaymen were just out of reach in the darkness, or indeed what else was sitting just beyond her vision, waiting.

Suddenly they came to a stop outside a door.

"This is the one," said Bess, pulling out a key. She glanced at Evelyn who noticed a look flicker across her face, just for a moment then it was gone. Evelyn couldn't quite place the emotion: guilt? Sadness? She wasn't sure, but Bess swung open the door and led her into the room.

As with the rest of the house, this room had been abandoned some time ago; it was dark and musty and only a fraction of daylight pierced the shutters on the windows. Bess started to light some of the candles and Evelyn realised that this room wasn't quite as dusty as the others. The walls had been painted a soft, powder blue and there were no sheets hiding furniture. There was a dolls house in the corner, a white rocking horse and a wooden chest, which Evelyn imagined to be full of dolls and toys as if a little girl had left, just a moment ago. She noticed a large bed with clean sheets and wondered if this was where Bess had been sleeping.

"Will you be alright if I go and fetch some food?" Evelyn nodded and Bess left, softly locking the door behind her.

She wandered over to the window, hoping that somehow it might offer an easy escape, a simple way to end the mess. She hadn't heard any sounds from outside, but still she hoped she might be in the centre of a town, somewhere she could attract attention to herself and be rescued. But the shutters were nailed closed and she couldn't see anything through the cracks.

She looked around the rest of the room—as well as the toys there was a chest of drawers and a small table and chairs, there were plenty of other rooms in the house, it seemed odd that Bess should have chosen a nursery, but then she considered it might be the only room with a key. The bed looked inviting, she felt exhausted but she resisted the urge to crawl into it, taking a seat instead and resting her eyes.

Just for a moment.

EIGHT

She awoke to Bess setting down a plate of bread, cheese, and fruit on the table. She smiled and thanked her but didn't feel up to eating, her head still hurt and her stomach was uneasy. But she did want to find out more about Bess, about this quiet girl sitting opposite her. Evelyn remembered the night she'd come to her room, 'was it only last night?' She'd seemed so intriguing, so mysterious, and now she found herself unsettled by how little she knew about Bess.

"So how did you come to be part of this gang?" she asked.

"It's a long story," Bess replied, shaking her head, and pulling out the soft insides from a bread roll.

"Well I suppose I have time to hear it."

Bess sighed and leaned back in her chair. She stared at the candlelight, before beginning.

"We all met in London," she started. "Jim was a butcher from Cheapside; Johnny was a sheep rustler and used to get lamb and mutton from Essex. They had a good thing going but something went wrong and now they have to stay out of the city for a while…"

"And the other one…?"

"Oh, Charlie," Bess smiled and Evelyn started to wonder how close they were to one another. "Poor Charlie, he's a good man but he owes a good amount of people a good amount of money. As far as I know he's entitled to a large inheritance but until his father dies, he has nothing." Bess threw the hollowed-out bread crust onto her plate.

"And you?"

"Me?" Bess looked up at her and frowned. "I don't have an inheritance, or a trade. I had nothing in London. Worse than nothing…" She stopped and looked back at the candle. "This is the only way I can get out of there."

She said the words like a mantra, as if she had repeated them to herself every day, telling herself, 'this is the only way.'

"The only way you can get out of where?"

Bess was starting to open up and Evelyn desperately wanted to know more; she pushed away the dark cloud of sleep that pushed against her temples. Bess met her gaze for a moment.

"You don't look well," she said. "Here, lie down for a while."

Evelyn felt herself being eased out of the chair.

"No, I'm alright," she heard herself say, but Bess didn't

listen and Evelyn didn't resist. As soon as she lay down she felt her consciousness slip away.

***

She was pulled out of her sleep by a constant tapping. She turned over, trying to remember where she was and who could be knocking for her at this hour. She opened her eyes briefly and saw Bess unlocking the door. She closed her eyes again, remembering. She wasn't at home, it wasn't morning. She was kidnapped, held hostage; she'd run away from everything she'd known into the arms of a woman that had betrayed her within the hour. She curled up on herself and lay with her eyes closed listening to the hushed conversation at the door.

"What is it?" Bess asked.

"It's William, he wants to see you." Evelyn almost gasped, that was the same voice she'd heard earlier, she knew it was Charlie and he must be talking about her William. William must have come looking for her! He and her father must have realised that something wasn't right when she didn't return on the first carriage and now he was here and he was going to free her!

"What? Why?" Bess stepped out of the room but left the door slightly ajar.

"He doesn't trust any of us, I said you'd go and meet him."

"I've got to go to the Harker's' tonight."

"You can go on to theirs from the White Hart—"

Evelyn was delighted. She realised the engagement was more than a business venture for William: he cared for her. He hadn't waited a single day before riding out to track her down; he must have discovered what had happened, located the gang and was, at this very moment, negotiating the ransom in that pub, in the 'White Hart'. She wondered if he would follow them here and gallantly rescue her.

She felt Bess gently shaking her arm.

"Wake up," she said. Evelyn slowly opened her eyes and looked up at her, waiting to be told that she was set free and could go home.

"I have to go away, for a few hours," said Bess.

"When will you be back?"

"Some time tomorrow."

"Tomorrow?" she said, horrified. Bess was going to leave her at the mercy of her gang for a whole night. "Why can't I go with you now?" she pleaded.

Bess sat down on the bed and looked at her.

"Now isn't the time," she said. "I will get you free but if I go too quickly then all of this will be for nothing and neither of us will be safe."

"I can protect you, you can come back with me and we can make sure that you're safe!"

"It's not that easy—"

"It is that easy!"

Bess shook her head and left the room. She didn't look back as she closed the door.

Evelyn was infuriated. Why did Bess insist on bowing to the demands of this gang? She had seemed so strong and proud but Evelyn realised that inside Bess was just a frightened and greedy little girl. Well if Bess couldn't help her escape, then perhaps William would, all she had to do was wait.

Only she didn't know how long she would have to wait for. She didn't know if he would ride to her rescue. She didn't know how he was going to find out where she was being kept. He may be forced to negotiate the ransom and gain her release, but that could take days. In the meantime, she was stuck here, at the mercy of a gang of men, at the mercy of Johnny.

Evelyn stared at the window shutters. The wood looked old and weak; she would be able to open them by force. She was only on the first floor; she could jump from the window and just walk down to the village.

Suddenly there was a key in the lock.

She sat up, expecting Bess, but it was Charlie, Bess' 'good man'. He wasn't wearing his mask and in the candlelight, he was relatively handsome, his hair was light, he wore a broad smile and he bowed to her, awkwardly.

"I'm here to watch over you, Miss Evelyn."

"Oh" said Evelyn, glancing back at the window "thank you."

He walked over to the fireplace and leaned against it. He fished out a clay pipe from his pocket and slowly started replacing the tobacco.

"If there is anything I can get you, do let me know." He said eventually.

She thought for a moment, he was polite, well-mannered and Bess had indicated that he was, or had been, a gentleman. Evelyn wondered just how much of a gentleman he was.

"Yes, there is," she said, "is there any chance I could... have a wash?"

"I don't know..." He was clearly surprised by her request. "I don't see why not. I'll be back in a moment." He left the room, careful to lock the door behind him and Evelyn crept over to the window.

It was hard to tell in the dim light but the wood looked weak; she pulled at one of the handles and it came off in her hand. There were heavy footsteps on the landing. Quickly, she threw the wooden handle in the fireplace and sat on the edge of the bed.

Awkwardly, Charlie carried a bucket through the door and placed it by the hearth with a few rags. He looked up at her for a moment and she wondered if he intended to stay.

"I'll leave you to it," he said quietly before shuffling out the door. She stayed perfectly still as she listened to his footsteps fade across the house. Then she ran to the wooden shutters.

Evelyn felt around the edges of the wood, trying to slide her hands underneath. She found a small gap and squeezed her fingers under the frame. Something brushed against her finger tips and she almost screamed as she yanked her fingers out. Evelyn struggled with the thought of spiders, hundreds of them swarming behind the frame, all ready and waiting for her to yank it open so they could leap out and crawl all over her face.

"Come on, Evie," she whispered to herself. Taking a deep breath, she eased her fingers under the shutter again and steadied herself. Then she gave it a heave. She wrenched it again and again and again and it flew open, banging hard against the wall. She stood rooted to the spot, waiting for a reaction from someone in the house.

Silence.

Relieved, she stepped forward to the window. It was much later than she'd thought, nearly sunset, she must have slept for a good few hours but the sky was still bright blue and the sun lit up the countryside. There were empty fields in all directions, the harvesters had gone home and left the remainder of their work for the morning. A few yards from the house, standing alone in one of the pastures was a sycamore tree, its leaves swayed softly in the breeze. Suddenly the image of Bess swinging from one of its outstretched branches entered her head, pale and lifeless, hung for betraying her precious gang.

She shook the thought from her mind and reassured herself that as Bess was nothing to do with her escape, the gang could not harm her. But there was no way she could stay alone in this eerie old house at their mercy. She had to run.

She carefully unlocked the window and tried to lift the lower pane, it was stuck, and for a moment she thought somebody had nailed the windows shut, but with a wriggle it came loose and let in the warm summer air.

Leaning out she saw it was a sheer drop and closed her eyes for a moment before gaining the courage to slip out onto the sill. She sat in the window staring down at the ground.

'It's too far!' she thought. She was usually comfortable with heights, enjoyed them even, but at the thought of having to jump twenty feet to the ground, she suddenly felt dizzy. She decided to turn and lower herself down, getting as close to the ground as possible.

The edge of the sill was narrow and uncomfortable; she had to grab hold of the window frame to steady herself. Flakes of rotten wood came loose in her fingers as she awkwardly twisted around and wriggled ungracefully onto her front.

She gave the room a last glance. For a brief moment, she saw the rocking horse, the little dolls' house, the unkempt bed, the table with the plate of food, and then she lowered herself to hang from the window. Gripping tightly with both hands she stayed there for a few seconds, unable to pull herself up and unwilling to let go. Her fingers were slipping and began to hurt. She looked down and quickly looked back up again.

"Oh God!" she cried, and dropped.

NINE

Evelyn stared at the sky.

She was stunned, winded and her ankle hurt. She wondered if she should have taken her shoes off before clambering out the window. Falling to the ground in heeled boots had not been her finest moment. She found herself hoping that no one had seen. Not so much for fear of being caught but for the ungainly manner in which she'd hit the ground.

She forced herself up onto her feet and leaned against the wall. She was at the back of the house; fields stretched out before her, acres, and acres of bare, open fields. There was nowhere to hide.

She crept along to the corner and peered around to the front of the house. There was a barn backing onto a newly tilled field and, just beyond that a hedgerow, stretching off into the distance. She knew that must be the road.

She would have to creep behind the barn and get to the road without being seen. From there she would have the high hedgerows to keep her from view. It would be risky but she could get further, faster.

Keeping her back to the wall, she crept along the side of the house, crawling in places in order to stay under the windows. She knew they were boarded up but she didn't want to take the chance.

She heard the laughter of the highwaymen from somewhere inside and imagined them sitting around the fire, planning what they were going to do to her.

Holding her breath, she edged forwards. At the corner, she peered round the wall to check the front of the house.

There was a cobbled yard surrounded by outbuildings with a path that led away from the house and joined up with the road. There was no one there. There were a few birds but the rest of the world was silent.

She took a deep breath and left the comfort of the shadows. Skirting around the cobbles, she ran towards the old barn and slammed her back against it, before turning to look at the front of the house.

If anyone so much as glanced out a window, they would see her. She urged herself to move, edging along the wall to hide behind the far corner. She kept both eyes on the empty black windows of the house, her pulse racing as step by painfully slow step, she finally managed to slip out of sight behind the barn.

There was no path. She was standing in freshly overturned soil—it clung to her boots like damp clay. Leaning on the barn wall, she started her journey towards the road.

With each step, she collected more and more mud until it encased her boots. She hoisted up her skirts and, as each foot became heavier, she swung them forward, using their weight to cast her stride further. By the time, she reached halfway she was exhausted and took a moment to catch her breath.

She was cold, tired and her shoes were ruined.

"How did I get here?" she asked herself and started to laugh.

It had been barely a week since she'd attended one of the finest balls in Cambridge, held partly in her honour, she'd been seen sporting the latest fashion and heard that Lady Huxley herself had been practically inconsolable with jealousy at the sight of her Parisian lace. Now here she was, standing ankle deep in mud, in a field, in the dark, with her skirts hoisted above her knees.

'Pull yourself together, woman!' she thought and shook off the mud.

She sighed and started her journey again. When she reached the far side of the barn, she had to rest again. She peered around the corner, she was a good distance from the house but they could still see her if they looked. She was just a few feet from the main road where she prayed the hedgerow would protect her from view.

Giving the house one last glance, she made a run for it. For a few seconds, she felt as though she were in a dream, a dream where no matter how fast you run, you never move. But then she was at the hedge and on the road. She darted around the corner and wondered which way to go.

The day before, when she'd been walking, she'd seen a hamlet in a valley. She wondered if that was the village where William was staying. She couldn't have been carried far from that glen, after all, it seemed unlikely that she would have been made to walk all that way if they weren't making sure she was getting closer to the hideout. So, she reasoned, the valley may hold the village where William is staying. Even if she was wrong, she thought, there were bound to be people there and she could ask about the 'White Hart'.

'Besides,' she thought, starting her journey, 'it was easier to walk downhill.'

Gradually the sun went down and it began to get colder and darker, only the cold light of the full moon showed her the way.

Occasionally a cloud would drift across the bright, white orb and the world would be plunged into blackness, a black so thick and absolute that Evelyn wondered if she would ever see again, but the moment would pass and gradually the moon would once again bestow on her its hollow, silver glow.

As she wandered down that lonely path she allowed herself the intense satisfaction of victory. She had successfully escaped her captors. She! She had been severely underestimated by those fools. She giggled as she imagined their faces when they eventually troubled themselves to check on her. She pictured them running around the house and across the fields trying to track her down, wondering how she'd managed to escape.

BANG!

She stopped dead. She was sure it was a bang, loud and clear on the soft night air. She listened, unsure where it had come from, unsure whether she'd imagined it.

She heard a shout, a yell. A loud booming yell,

definitely a man and definitely angry.

She stood rooted to the spot. Could she hide? Could she scramble into the hedgerow, would they go past her?

There was another yell.

She decided to run.

She picked up her skirts and fled downhill. Her feet were light on the downward slope. She struggled to keep her balance. She could hear further shouts in the distance and another bang followed a few moments later.

She was struggling with the weight of her skirts, her legs ached from the trek across the mud, she had a sharp pain in her side and her chest was heavy.

It was only a few moments before she had to stop.

She tried to keep breathing but she doubled over coughing. Crouching in the middle of the road she tried to force the breath back into her chest.

There was no shouting. Part of her hoped they'd stopped looking. But with horrible realisation it dawned on her.

They'd split up.

With two roads and three men, she knew at least one of them was running toward her. She just prayed it wasn't the one with the loaded gun.

'Why did I run?'

With the ache in her side and her ankles still painful from the fall, she stood and carried on running. The clouds passed in front of the moon and the blackness enveloped her. She kept running.

The hill levelled out and she jogged along, before coming to a stop at crossing. Another road headed upward to her right, the other kept on straight ahead. She knew it would be wise to go up the hill as they would be unlikely to follow her. But that was only if one person had come after, perhaps two, or even all three had followed her down this path. Evelyn started pace on the spot, dancing in frustration. She was too tired to think. Too cold to weigh-up the pros and cons.

Suddenly she heard voices. At least two of them were right behind her. She didn't have time to think. She needed to hide. She rushed to the edge of the road and scrambled up onto the bank, squeezing through a gap in the hedge. There was a field: it hadn't been harvested and the shadows of the plants, like a black ocean of snakes, stretched out before her. At the far edge of the field was a wood. She glanced behind her, just as the highwaymen turned the corner. She gasped and fell backwards into the field.

TEN

Disorientated and in pain, she forced herself to her feet. She could see the woods in the distance and took off in their direction but she barely had a head start. Her heart was pounding. Fear was running through her veins and she pushed herself to run faster. She hoisted up her skirts and sped across the middle of the field. The earth here was hard and dry between rows of knee-high plants; she ran between them and as each heeled shoe pounded against the ground the shock reverberated up to her knee.

She heard shouting. She knew they were following her, but couldn't bring herself to turn around. She forced herself to move faster but the trees were so far away.

BANG!

One of them had taken a pot shot at her. The shock

made her stumble slightly but she barely stopped. She kept focused on the trees and kept running.

Just a few more seconds.

Her chest was getting heavy and it hurt to breathe. She could hear them behind her. She knew they were getting closer and she ran. She knew if they took another shot they would hit her. Her chest was screaming. But it was just a few yards.

Just a couple of yards.

She was beyond the tree line and darted right. She skipped over roots, and through nettles. She was torn at by brambles but she knew she had to go deeper. She ran in zigzags and hoped they couldn't follow her tracks. She leapt over a ditch and nearly fell. She scrambled onto her feet and kept running.

She came to a clearing. There was barely any light, but she could see a foot path and darted along it. It veered downhill, it was easier to run but as it became steeper, she nearly toppled and had to slow down.

She could see a huge oak tree rising out of the dark, running over to it she hid behind its trunk. She looked back the way she had come, gasping for air. There was no one there. But it was dark and a man could easily be hidden in the shadows.

As her breathing slowed, she closed her eyes and listened to the sounds of the forest. There were a few birds singing into the night and she could hear faint rustling. Heavy footsteps in the leaves.

She started to panic. She couldn't outrun anyone and didn't know where the rustling had come from. She could end up running straight into them. She looked at the trunk of the oak tree. It was gnarled and twisted with a few knot holes and huge branches reaching up into the forest canopy.

She hadn't climbed a tree since she was a girl and even then, it had only been when she was with her father; her mother and governess had no tolerance for that type of behaviour.

She reached up and grabbed hold of a branch, finding a foothold she boosted herself up. She reached out with her other hand, clawing along the bark for a knot hole until she got a firm grip and then pulled. Gradually she eased herself up the trunk. She was sure she could hear him now, crashing through the woods breaking twigs and branches as he searched for her.

Evelyn grabbed hold of a huge branch and heaved herself up onto it. She wasn't nearly as nimble as she had been and her legs flailed out. She shifted onto her stomach and wriggled along it. She needed to stand up to climb higher but she didn't think she was capable. She just hoped it was dark enough for her to be hidden.

She tried to be quiet. Tried not to breathe as she listened. He was coming from behind and she tried to crane her neck to see him in the dark. There was a shadow. A great hulking shadow, blundering through the woods.

She held her breath and waited for him to pass by. It was Johnny. His unmistakably huge figure was following the same footpath she'd found. He was going to pass by her tree. He was using his musket to beat the bushes. Suddenly he stopped and stood perfectly still.

He was listening. She held her breath and tried to somehow stop her heart from beating. If he glanced up to his right he would see her. He was just a few feet away. She wondered if he could smell her, like a wolf smells its prey.

She felt a tickling at her chest. She hoped it wasn't a spider. She wasn't sure what she would do if a spider crawled across her face. She stayed quiet and hoped.

Suddenly he moved. He turned slowly on the spot, peering into the darkness. She prayed he would go, just go, in any direction. He came full circle and faced her direction. He took a few cautious steps forward. She felt the tickling on her chest again and nearly cried out but clenched her teeth to prevent it. Just then her locket tumbled out of her ripped bodice. It swung a few inches from his ear as he peered into the shadows below her.

She daren't move to catch it. Even if he didn't see the locket, then he would definitely hear her move. She closed her eyes. She couldn't watch. There was nothing she could do but pray.

He moved away. She heard blundering through the trees and as she opened her eyes she saw his shadow prowling off into the darkness.

When she did start to breathe again she sobbed in relief.

She wasn't sure what to do next. Should she stay in the tree all night and hope they wouldn't pass this way again? Or should she make a run for it, knowing that she could run head-first into Johnny?

Then she thought of William. He would be pacing in his room waiting for news of her, worried sick about her, desperate to see her again. She knew that as soon as she reached him she would be safe.

Slowly she eased herself back along the branch towards the trunk and tried to stand. It wasn't easy to stand in a tree in heeled boots but she held on tightly and hoped she wouldn't fall. From her vantage point she could see a few distant lights scattered in the darkness. She thought they must be from outlying cottages and decided to make her way towards one of them and ask if they knew the way to the 'White Hart'.

She closed her eyes and listened to the dark, trying to pick out any rustling from nearby highwaymen. She knew she was safe in the tree and wanted to avoid putting herself in danger, but at the same time she couldn't just wait in the tree forever.

She crawled onto her front and swung her legs down, trying to gain a foothold. There was nothing for her to grip to and her feet flailed wildly as her grasp slipped from the branch. She tried to claw her way back up in a panic but she didn't have the strength.

She hit the ground with a thump.

She lay in the undergrowth for a moment catching her breath. She'd never fallen off so much in so little time. She hauled herself off the floor and leaned on the oak tree. Her backside hurt but she was determined to ignore it and continue with her daring escape. She closed her eyes and tried to remember which direction she had seen the lights. It had been to her right, definitely to her right. As quietly as she could, she took off through the woods.

She had to walk slowly, there was only just enough light for her to see shapes in the darkness and she wanted to avoid walking straight into a bramble patch.

She was forced off course a few times and had no clue if she was still heading in the right direction or just going around in circles. She was exhausted and cursed herself for not eating when she'd had the chance. It was getting colder and darker all the time, her head was still pounding, her muscles ached and her feet hurt.

She had never realised how much of her body needed to work when it took one simple footstep, her legs, thighs, back and shoulder all ached in unison as she scrabbled onward in the dark. She took hold of branches and trunks to help pull her along through the woods.

She tried to concentrate on William, on seeing his face when she came into the Inn. He would order her food and drink and a warm bed, he would rush out in the morning to buy her new clothes and then he would burn her travelling dress. He would take care of her and make sure she got home safely and warmly. But as she kept on clawing and scraping a path through the woods she couldn't stop the tears of frustration and fatigue welling up.

She let them fall.

ELEVEN

Eventually the trees eased off and she came to a patch of stinging nettles swaying in the moonlight. They stretched ahead a few yards and hit a dry-stone wall, although the wall was only a few feet high it was too dark to see what was beyond it. There could be a field or a garden or a road or a gang of musket-laden highwaymen, but she decided that whatever it was, it was better than the woods.

Carefully she edged forward, using her boots to squish down the nettles and create a path. She wrapped her skirts around her legs; her stockings went as far as her knee, but she was stung in spite of them.

Finally, she grabbed hold of the wall and hoisted herself on to it, pulling a few loose stones into the nettle patch as she did so. Groping around in the dark, she managed to swing first one and then the other foot over, she eased herself down the other side and cried out as she scratched along the back of her legs. But she was out of the woods. She allowed herself a moment of exhilarated relief before she took in her surroundings.

She was on a road; one way led down into the valley and then wound its way back up the hill and into the darkness. She decided to take her chance on the downhill path and it was a pure relief to be free from nettles and brambles and unexpected roots. She would have skipped had she not had blisters.

Even with the full moon clear and at its full height, the road before her was dark and imposing. She started to wish she had stayed behind. At least in the house she had known what the danger was.

As she turned a corner she saw a twinkling of light in the distance, without a second thought she ran towards it. Her pace slowed as she came upon a little walled garden with a wooden gate. The wall was only as high as her knees and the garden beyond contained a strange assortment of shadowy plants, some in squared off patches and others in tall rows. The gate was at the head of a path, which ran down the centre like the aisle of a village church, with its attentive patrons all gazing towards an altar.

Evelyn stood at the gate for a moment. The garden was dark and intimidating but she felt a warmth pull at her from the tiny light; like a moth she was entranced and opened the little gate.

As she drew closer she could make out the cottage's silhouette. The thatched roof overhung the front of the house like the fringe on an unkempt dog, the light had come from one of the windows, the other was dark, giving the impression that the cottage was winking at her. There was an empty bucket and a pair of boots left at the little door, and the little iron knocker beckoned to her.

Evelyn imagined being received by the joyous, friendly country folk that inhabited this little piece of their own merry England. She imagined the family gathered around the fire recounting their day, they would invite her to sit with them and share their supper, before the man of the house would insist on walking her down to the inn. He would protect her from harm, defeating any marauding highwaymen with his superior skills with a musket, and make sure she arrived safely and without incident. She would introduce him to William, who would give him a crown or even a guinea for his trouble; he would then bring it back to his family who would all applaud him for his decision to open the door to a stranger in the night.

But she hesitated.

She glanced at the window, beaming its light out to the world like a beacon, she crept towards it. There was no covering and she could see right into the little room. The light came from the fire at the hearth; a large black cooking pot was hanging on the grate; a few pieces of clothing were held up to dry and a woman sat on a rocking chair with her back to the window. But what caught Evelyn's eye was the man: he was seated in the chair by the fire, his bare feet splayed out to catch the warmth of the hearth and on his lap, curled up with her head resting against his shoulder and her thumb in her mouth was a little girl sleeping on her daddy.

She didn't want to disturb them, she didn't want to pull that father away from his little girl and drag him into her sorry state of affairs. She had always looked at the simple life of country folk with envy. Their simple cares and worries, their minor achievements, and their bliss of ignorance. But she had always gone home to her estate and her servants and her books. As she stared at that family, looked through their little window from the outside, she saw their warmth, their happiness and their peace and she felt genuine envy, real, bitter envy and it hurt.

She would ask someone else, someone who suited her miserable situation. Or perhaps she would ask no one. She would find a hovel somewhere and set up a new life as a crone with a few cats and a stick.

She turned and fled downhill.

As she trudged through the darkness she became aware that she was passing more cottages. She could make out few scattered buildings up ahead and realised she was just a few feet from civilisation.

But clear on the night air she could here shouts and cries, many more voices this time. She stopped dead in the road.

She couldn't run. Maybe she should just give herself up. Bess had said that she wouldn't be hurt, the ransom was too important to them. Maybe she should just hand herself over, she could stop falling off things and running through things and go back to that bed and that plate of food. Bess would be back in the morning and then she would be taken to William and all this would be over.

But as she listened she realised there was music and, although it was difficult to hear, the voices seemed to be singing and not shouting at all. Cautiously, she continued into the village.

The buildings were all timber framed, ancient and

rickety, with misshapen roofs and unmatched windows. A few of them had large front windows and signs indicating a bakery or a butcher's. The singing was coming from a large inn, a new brick building and the largest building in the village. It lay on the other side of a small stream running through the green. All the windows, even the ones on the first floor, were lit up and she could just about make out the sign, a painting of a white deer.

"White Hart!"

She almost cried. She'd made it.

She ran towards the inn, crossing the bridge, and barely pausing for breath before she burst through the door.

She was hit by a wall of stifling air which stank of sweat and tobacco. The room was filled with laughter and people and she took a few moments to adjust. The singing was discordant and confused and although the music was joyful she could barely hear it over the chaotic noise of people. There was a woman dancing a jig on a table surrounded by a rowdy group of singers swinging their cups with no concern for their drink or the floor. There was a fire roaring in the grate at the far side of the room, which served only to add to the heat and the smell, there were lanterns and candles but their light couldn't fend of the dinginess of the dark walls and yellowed ceilings. There were people sitting on tables and standing on chairs, in every corner there were couples, but despite her sudden entrance and remarkable appearance, no one seemed to be aware of her.

She wondered why William had chosen such a place to stay but realised he must have been forced into such places in search of her captors. She fought her way to the bar and caught the attention of a bald, red faced man in an apron standing arms folded, watching the crowd with faint amusement.

"Do you have a Mr William Barrington here?" she shouted above the noise. He seemed a little startled and leaned towards her; she repeated her question.

"Mr Barrington, is he here?" He shook his head and pointed to his ear. "William? Is William Barrington staying here?"

The barman nodded, said something she didn't catch and pointed to the ceiling.

"Second!" he shouted, holding up two fingers. "Second on the left!"

As soon as she caught the words she was gone, she thought he shouted after her but she didn't care. She'd look in every room in the building if she had to. She knew he was here, she knew he'd come. She found the stairs easily enough and even though she could still hear and smell the bar, it was a relief to be out of the crowd.

Second on the left he'd said, and there it was, an unassuming wooden door. Her door back to freedom, her door out of the mad world she'd been living in the past few days, back to Abberton, back to her garden, back to her father. She didn't even mind the prospect of getting back in a coach.

She grabbed the handle and took a breath.

A moment of doubt crept across her, doubt that he was there, doubt that he had come to rescue her, doubt that he would ever come to rescue her. Suddenly, she thought all of her running, and falling and climbing trees, her daring and brilliant escape, had been in vain and she would be alone, with no money and nowhere to go.

"Please let it be him," she said, and opened the door.

William was there, sat at a table, a piece of bread raised to his mouth. He froze as he caught sight of Evelyn. He was everything she remembered, the smart dress, the deep brown eyes, he wasn't wearing his wig but she thought his unruly mop of black hair only served to make him more dashing. Her stomach flipped, she couldn't believe her good luck! The remarkable fortune that had led her to his door, she wanted to yell and scream and shout his name—

"Billy! Help me get in this flaming corset. They're a bugger to get tight." The words broke Evelyn's trance, she looked across as the speaker came through from an adjoining room. Dressed in flowing red skirts, with bare arms and her long, dark hair loose about her shoulders, Bess took a moment to register that Evelyn was standing at the door.

Niamh Murphy

TWELVE

She turned and ran.

Back down the stairs, through the crowded pub and out into the night air.

She didn't wait to see if they came after her, she didn't care. She no longer felt the blisters on her feet or her aching limbs, she just ran and carried on running.

She was running without direction, through the small streets and alleyways of the village. The harder she ran, the further from her mind she could push the image of William and Bess.

With her chest heaving she couldn't cry, and with her feet moving she couldn't collapse into a miserable heap.

But her body was only capable of so much and as she climbed the slope leading out of the village she started to slow.

Suddenly she was grabbed. A hand enveloped her mouth before she could scream. Strong arms held her and she was pulled to the side of the road and forced through a wooden door into a shed.

She was slammed against a wall. The hand stayed firmly against her mouth and she went to lash out, but as her captor leaned towards the small window, a moonbeam fell across her profile. It was Bess. Evelyn held back, surprised.

Satisfied that no one had followed them, Bess removed her hand from Evelyn's mouth.

"What are you doing here? How did you get out?" she hissed.

"How dare you?" Evelyn hissed back. "What were you doing?" She felt herself beginning to cry and held back, she didn't want Bess to know how much she hurt.

"It's not what you think!"

"Is that why I couldn't come with you?" She ignored the highwaywoman's lies, the picture was becoming clearer in her head, the deceit, the seduction. She should never have even been tempted by such a woman. She was disgusted at herself and humiliated, ashamed that she should have been fooled so easily.

"Evelyn –"

"How long did it take you to get him into bed? An hour? Two hours? And that whole time—" Her voice was starting to rise, screeching in a hysteria she couldn't contain.

Bess grabbed Evelyn and covered her mouth.

"Listen to me!" she whispered.

"Why should I?" she replied, throwing off the girl's hand. "Why should I do anything you say? Why should I trust you? You're just a whore! A FILTHY, LYING, CHEATING, STEALING—!"

"He's my brother!"

"What?" Evelyn stopped. She wriggled out of Bess' grip the hatred fell away to shock for a moment. "What?" she repeated.

"William is my brother." Saying the words again didn't make it easier for Evelyn to comprehend.

"How?" She stared at Bess in bewilderment trying to take in the revelation. "How can he be?"

"I shouldn't have said anything." Bess closed her eyes and rubbed her temples.

"Goddammit, Bess! How can you be his sister? This makes no sense!" The hatred was coming back, more lies, lies upon lies and compounded with lies. She was caged in. Bess stood over her in the small, stuffy, animal-smelling goat-shed; she needed to get out, she needed to breathe.

"I know. I'm sorry."

Bess' voice was soft, slow, there was a tenderness in it that still tugged at Evelyn. But her weakness only made her angrier.

"Bugger sorry!" she shouted. She was feeling claustrophobic and her heart was beating too fast; she wanted to take deep breaths but the air in the shed tasted foul. She reached for the door. "I need to get out of here."

Bess pulled her back.

"Please, you must listen to me!"

"I don't have to listen to any of your mad lies, I should never have gone with you, never have trusted you. I don't know what I was thinking, I was mad, it's all mad, all of this is just madness!"

"Please, Evelyn, he's looking for you!"

"William? Well good, I think I should give him a piece of my mind." She moved to the door but once again Bess pulled her back.

"You're not listening to me, Evie. It's him, it's Bill, he's behind all this: he planned it. He's the gang leader—he created the gang to kidnap you. If he finds you, if he finds out you know what he's done... I... I don't know what he'll do."

Bess was desperate, there was panic in her voice and she clung tightly to Evelyn's arm, but none of what she was saying made sense and Evelyn was starting to become frightened.

"You're deranged," she whispered.

"I'm not deranged." She let go. "I just need you to believe me. He has planned all this... everything, the proposal, the robbery, the kidnap... everything."

"But how...? Why?"

"For money. Why else?"

Despite herself, Evelyn was being drawn in.

"But William has money." She thought of the clothes he wore, the places he visited, his friends, his connections. "He's in business, in trade. He's been investing in the ships going out of Bristol for months—"

"There is no business, no ships, no imports. Nothing! He's been taking everything your father invested... just ...taking it."

Evelyn stared at her. In the dim moonlight, she could see her crumpled red dress was only half tied and the laces hung from her bodice, her dark hair hadn't been pinned and was loose about her shoulders, she looked wild, untamed, and beautiful. Her dark eyes were pleading with Evelyn to believe her but nothing made sense, her story was mad and fanciful.

"But William was going to invest." Evelyn said slowly, as if explaining to a child. "My father said that William was going to invest in the business, a great deal of money, he said—"

"I know," said Bess "That's why we needed money! There was no other way to obtain such a huge investment, don't you see?"

"So, you kidnapped me?"

"William thought your father would be too proud to go for help and he would willingly give over a ransom for you. William volunteered to hand it over to the kidnappers. But of course, he would keep the ransom and still set you free. Then he could then use the money as the investment..."

"And my father would never know..."

Evelyn thought about her father, her poor, foolish, trusting father and she realised, with despair, that it was true. She wondered how much money he'd given to William, how much of their estate had already been lost.

"And you knew all of this from the start?"

"Yes," Bess said quietly.

Evelyn wondered if she'd heard shame in her voice.

"How could you?" She felt disgusted—robbing a stage coach was one thing but it was only now she saw the depths this highwaywoman was willing to plummet to satisfy her greed.

"We had never meant it to get this far!" she said. "Bill never suspected that your father would ask for an investment upon marriage, we both believed he would be getting the dowry. William had planned everything in such detail, we were so close and then... an investment. We didn't know what to do... then we heard someone raving about a kidnap that had gone off without a hitch and William... he just went for it. We were so close, and now..." Bess looked straight at Evelyn. "Now we've lost everything."

"You are nothing but a thief..."

"It wasn't meant to be like this—"

"It all makes sense now." Evelyn laughed as the truth started to sink in "The days he'd come over and they'd talk business for hours... I should have seen it. He was so friendly, so nice, so charming... people try to get away from my father, William sought him out... But what were you doing half-dressed in his room?"

Bess hesitated before answering.

"We're going to a ball," she said quietly.

"A ball?"

"At the Harker's' estate."

"You were going to leave me in that house with those men while you went to a ball?" Evelyn was tired of surprises, tired of the running, tired of everything. "And is it normal for your brother to dress you?"

"Well I don't have anyone else! And you can't do these things up on your own, look at it!"

Bess spun round to show the back, the laces half-tied; Evelyn almost laughed at how pathetic she seemed, but it suddenly struck her how alone Bess really was. The woman, who had seemed so strong and adventurous, leading a gang of rogues to stop coaches, was suddenly a lost and lonely girl.

Evelyn couldn't help reaching out; it was dark, but there was still enough light to see the laces. She straightened them and began to tighten the bodice.

"I've ruined everything," Bess whispered to herself.

Evelyn was quiet—she didn't know how to comfort her captor and she wasn't sure if she wanted to.

"I shouldn't have come to your room that night, I shouldn't have got involved, I shouldn't have persuaded Charlie to keep you untied, I shouldn't have told you everything, I shouldn't even be talking to you now…"

"So, why are you?" Evelyn was cautious, worried that she might end up back in that bleak house with another musket wound to the head. Bess was quiet and Evelyn finished tightening the laces.

"I don't know."

Evelyn could hear a sob on her voice Bess turned but didn't look at Evelyn.

"I just… I don't …I don't want to hurt you. I want to protect you." She said each word slowly as if carefully placing it on the air between them.

"How can I even begin to trust you?" Evelyn said, recoiling. Bess breathed out slowly and looked up.

"I love you."

Evelyn was startled. Bess looked straight back towards her; there were fresh tears on her cheeks, but she didn't bother to wipe them away.

"I've loved you since the moment you said you'd rather stand. I don't know why, or how, I just know that I love you, and all I want, all I've wanted since I met you, is to just… be near to you, just be close, and just…oh God, I don't know… I'm sorry..." She was struggling to speak, and fresh tears were pouring out.

Evelyn was overwhelmed, she wanted to reach out, to hold her, to comfort her, but she was still so uncertain.

"We can't go back." She wanted to make it clear that if she was going to trust Bess, it was going to be on her terms. She wasn't going to allow herself to get pulled into whatever dark trade this woman had planned.

"I know," Bess replied, closing her eyes, and breathing out slowly. "I think Bill might kill us."

The words were said so coldly that Evelyn wondered if she was telling the truth. It sent a chill across her bones to think of murder being so lightly mentioned.

"Then perhaps we should hide." Evelyn was reluctant to go back into the woods or stay in the goat-shed but she knew they had few options.

"I know somewhere we could go." The words had come out so quickly that Evelyn instantly mistrusted them.

"How do I know you won't just take me back to them?" she asked.

"Please trust me." She held out her hand.

Evelyn looked at it. She was exhausted, dirty, hungry, and her head ached.

"Give me one good reason why I should go with you?"

"I don't have one." Bess' hand dropped. "I just want this to be over and I don't want anyone else to get hurt."

Evelyn felt helpless. It was only a few minutes ago that she had pinned all her hope on William, and now she was relying on the good word of a highwaywoman. She wanted to believe her, wanted to trust her, wanted to go with her wherever she was going and yet couldn't bring herself to. But she realised that there was no one else.

Evelyn sighed, knowing she was making a desperate mistake, and took Bess' hand.

"So, where is this hiding place?"

THIRTEEN

The barn was an ominous shadow towering up into the darkness. Evelyn wasn't convinced she wanted to go inside at all, let alone hide in there all night.

"What if somebody comes?" she whispered, as Bess led her up to the door.

"No one goes in a barn in the middle of the night, and we'll be gone long before anyone gets up." She glanced at Evelyn before grabbing the door. "Come on, it'll be fine."

She cursed herself, but cautiously followed Bess inside.

The barn was pitch black and a musty smell hung in the air, a mixture of oil, hay, and animals. She could hear the creaking of the wood against the light wind and the metal catch shutting as Bess slid the door closed. Evelyn felt her chest tighten—she wasn't usually afraid of the dark but in a foreign place, but with the gang on the loose she felt herself giving into fear.

"I can't see anything," she whispered, trying to keep the panic out of her voice.

"I know, it's alright. Hold on a moment."

She heard Bess strike a match, there was a flash and then nothing. Bess muttered under her breath and tried another.

"You're carrying matches?" she asked, surprised at Bess' resourcefulness.

"I carry them everywhere."

The next match stayed alight, and she watched Bess protect the small flame with her hand; the relief of having light swept through her and she began to calm down as Bess searched along the wall.

"What are you looking for?" she asked.

"Well if this was my barn," she replied, without breaking her search, "I'd keep a couple- yes, here we go." She reached up to a shelf with a small stack of candles and lit one with the last flicker of her match. "I'd keep a couple of candles out here and maybe… a lantern."

The candle threw out much more light and they could see a few small lanterns hanging from hooks along the wall. Bess reached up for one and placed the candle inside, cursing softly when a drop of wax landed on her hand.

"Well, let's look around," she said, putting her hand out for Evelyn to take.

The lantern threw an orange glow across the unfamiliar shapes and shadows in the darkness. There were tools lining the walls, forks and scythes of assorted sizes; there was a small empty cart leaning on its front and a stack of barrels in a corner. As they crept forward Evelyn could make out a hayloft, six feet or so off the ground and held up with a few wooden beams. The hay was piled high both in the hayloft and on the ground before them.

"It's not quite silk sheets but it will be more comfortable than a ditch. We're lucky; it looks like they only brought this in recently." Bess leant down and pressed her hand into the hay, as if testing a mattress. "What do you think?" She looked up, clearly delighted with their find.

"Will there be rats in it?" Evelyn asked.

"Rats?" The delight washed off Bess's face and she looked back at the hay with suspicion. "I don't think so; farmers have a lot of cats so we should be fine."

"What about spiders?"

"Spiders...? Well... cats eat spiders, so that should be fine too."

"Cats eat spiders?" Evelyn started to wonder just how easily lies came to Bess' lips.

"Yes, of course they do, and whatever they miss the owls get."

"There are owls in here?" Evelyn instinctively looked upwards.

"Probably. I don't know. Are you alright with this?"

Evelyn closed her eyes. She was not alright. The thought of spending the night in a rat-infested barn, with owl droppings and spiders, let alone the thought of the gang catching up with them at any moment, was not making her feel 'alright'. Bess squeezed her hand and she opened her eyes.

"Perhaps if we go up into the hayloft, it might be better," Evelyn said.

Bess looked up.

"Into the hayloft?"

"Yes. To get off the ground—it should be safer, shouldn't it?"

"Alright." She handed Evelyn the lantern and found the ladder leaning next to the wall.

"Do you want to go first?" When Evelyn shook her head, Bess breathed out slowly before climbing up and swinging herself in to the hayloft with ease. She reached down and Evelyn passed her the lantern before taking hold of the ladder herself. It wobbled slightly and she was wary of putting her full weight on it, but it was only a few steps to the top and Bess helped her up.

"Happier?" Bess asked. She nodded.

They made a snug little nest between a few bales, then lay in the darkness in their under-shirts, resting on their outer clothes to avoid the worst of the itching from the hay.

"We only have a few hours before sunrise," Bess whispered softly, inching closer and rested her head on Evelyn's shoulder

"Well we'd best get some sleep," she replied, keeping her voice even, but her heart was pounding. She could smell Bess's hair and wanted to reach out and touch her skin. Tentatively she felt for her hand in the darkness.

Bess turned slowly, her mouth just inches from Evelyn's.

"Goodnight," she whispered and leaned forward, brushing her lips against Evelyn's.

She couldn't help but pull Bess closer. Her hand moved across Bess' back, pulling her into a deep, fervent kiss. She licked the soft skin of her lips, gently biting, and caressing her, unable to let her go.

Suddenly Bess slid on top of her, running her hand along her thigh, squeezing as she gently rocked her hips.

Evelyn told herself it was just a kiss, just a long, powerful kiss, that she could stop at any moment, that she wasn't consumed by desire. But as she raised her hips to meet Bess', she pushed all other thoughts out of her mind.

She grabbed the soft, taut flesh of Bess' thighs, squeezing, massaging, and pulling them closer. She heard Bess cry out softly, her gentle rocking becoming more frantic.

Evelyn slowly pulled up Bess' under-shirt and gently reached underneath for the bare flesh of Bess' thigh, stroking the skin. But she wanted more, she needed more. She moved Bess onto her side, stroking the soft skin of her inner thigh before sliding her hand slowly upwards. Bess arched her back and gasped as Evelyn felt her, silken and wet, beneath her fingers.

They barely broke their kiss as Evelyn felt Bess' hand slide up her thigh and push softly against her and they gently writhed against one another.

She moaned as she felt Bess become more frenzied, her breathing hurried and she could no longer control herself as she cried out. Bess was rigid against her, biting her lip and moaning as her body shook and the last surge of ecstasy washed over her.

They held each other in the darkness, breathing heavily, unable to talk, unsure what to say.

Evelyn had never considered that she could feel something so powerful, something that had rushed through every inch of her body. She wondered if it was love.

She realised that had been what she had wanted from Bess the moment she'd seen her. She had wanted to be closer, always closer, and now she felt as though they had finally connected with one another, and she had found something in Bess that she had never found or even wanted in another person. She wanted to tell her, to say the words and explain how she felt.

Then she heard the latch, and the barn door opened.

Evelyn felt Bess stiffen against her and her arms held her tighter.

"I dunno, I haven't heard nothing." It was a deep voice, a man's voice but one that Evelyn didn't recognise.

"Well you never know." It was Johnny—the deep gruffness was unmistakable.

Her heart stopped.

He would be sure to search the hayloft, sure to find them there, together. A cold sweat swept across her as she thought of what he might do, how he might react. She wondered if Bess would be able to save her from harm or if she would be defenceless without her gun or her sword.

They had a lantern; the light glowed in the darkness but didn't reach them hidden between the bales. She heard the grinding of metal against the ground and wondered what they were doing.

She remembered the ladder; it was still against the hayloft. Would they see it? Would they know they were there?

She glanced at Bess and in the faint light she could see her face, impassive and unmoving and she wondered how she could be so calm, wondered if Bess had known they would come, had led her here to hand her over and had taken advantage of her. She couldn't ask. She could do nothing but lie in silence holding her breath and waiting for whatever was to come.

"I can get the dogs out if you want, John, Mary won't be happy about it but if it's a help…" There was a long pause, an age of a pause, while Johnny considered his options and Evelyn's fate hung in the balance.

"Nah," he said finally. "Did you say you got some rum going?"

"Oh yeah, I got some lovely stuff…" Their voices faded as the doors closed behind them. The girls strained their ears in the darkness, listening to their footsteps on the cobbles leading back up to the house.

Finally, Evelyn breathed out. Bess eased off her and rolled onto her side.

She lay in the darkness straining to hear further sounds, they may come back and check later, they may get drunk and set the dogs out after all. She didn't dare move, didn't dare allow herself to close her eyes.

It was a long night.

It was many hours before eventually Evelyn drifted off into an uncomfortable sleep.

She dreamt she was drowning. She had weights tied to her legs and was being pulled deeper and deeper into the ocean. She struggled desperately against the weights, trying to swim back towards the surface, back towards the light getting further and further away. All the while Bess was there—she was a mermaid and swum freely around Evelyn, she was beautiful and graceful. Evelyn tried to call out to her but no sound would come from her mouth. She wasn't sure if Bess was there to save her, or just to watch her drown. She struggled against the water, trying to hold her breath, trying to stop it from flooding her lungs. She reached out to Bess who stared back at her impassively as she fought, until finally she could hold her breath no longer and gulped in the water.

She awoke, startled from her uncomfortable sleep. The light was poking in through the cracks in the barn walls and it took her a while to remember where she was.

She turned, hoping to catch a glimpse of Bess still sleeping next to her, to try to gain some comfort from her. But she was alone.

Bess was gone.

FOURTEEN

Gathering her clothes together, Evelyn muttered angrily to herself and began to slowly dress. The hay was itchy and persistent in its attachment to her. She methodically shook out each garment, before awkwardly shifting about in the small space trying to put them on.

Dressing alone was always so much more difficult than having someone to help, and trying to make sure the laces were straight on the back of her corset was almost impossible. She concentrated hard on the task, refusing to allow herself to think of Bess.

To think of being abandoned and betrayed again.

She refused to let it enter her head, refused to remember the night before and how easily she had given in, how easily she had trusted Bess. She refused to acknowledge how much she had wanted to trust her, to believe in her and to be with her.

She refused to admit how hurt she was.

She tried to refuse.

But as she struggled with the awkward laces, her arms tired and unwilling to co-operate, she couldn't refuse any longer.

A tear spilled over her cheek, she bit her lip and steadied her jaw but she no longer had the strength and she gave in, sobbing into her hands.

She allowed herself the momentary weakness, before forcing herself to breathe steadily. She wiped the tears from her face.

She noticed Bess' mask. She'd kept it hidden in her bodice, and it was now sitting in the hay looking up at her. She decided to ignore it.

"Come on Evie," she said to herself. "Get out of this."

More determined after her lapse, Evelyn finished dressing. She decided that straight laces were the least of her worries—she was going to have to find the way to Bristol alone.

It shouldn't be too difficult: she would just keep walking until she found a town and then ask for directions. It would be simple.

Of course, she would just have to hope that she didn't go back in the direction of the village. Or the farmhouse. Or walk straight into one of the gang on the road.

She pushed those thoughts out of her mind and pulled on her stockings and boots. She took a long, deep breath and told herself that she was ready to tackle whatever the world was about to throw at her.

She noticed that Bess had at least been decent enough

to leave the ladder for her, but she refused to allow herself to thank the girl, even silently.

As soon as she was on the ground she placed the ladder back where they had found it and did the best job she could of brushing the remaining hay off her skirts. She wasn't sure of the time but the sun was up and she knew that there may well be an army of farmhands just outside the barn door.

She wondered how they would react to her, if they would believe her story or simply have her strung up for trespassing. She crept across the barn and opened the door, just by a sliver, looking out at the courtyard.

It was empty, and she felt brave enough to open it wider, until finally she could stick her head out and look around.

She could hear the birds happily chirping their dawn chorus but there was no other sound. No shouting or calling, or any other early morning 'farm noises' that she had expected to hear. The morning air was cool and the sun was only just warming the ground. A soft mist hung on the air and the world seemed at peace with itself.

She slipped out in to the yard and looked up at the timber-framed farmhouse. There were plenty of windows should anyone wish to look out and see her; she thought about knocking. She could explain her situation: the kidnap, the ransom, the escape. She could offer the household a reward for helping her and turning in William and the gang—she might even get some breakfast.

Then she thought about Bess, about her highwaywoman, swinging for her crimes, not from a tree but from gallows—a public hanging, a crowd cheering her death—and she hesitated.

The memory of the night before came back to her, how gentle she'd seemed, how honest. How they had held one another. She must have felt the same. It couldn't have been a lie. Could it?

Then she thought back to that first night, how easily Bess had held a pistol to her and the other passengers, how she'd led her into that glen, the state of undress she'd found her in with William.

She lied so easily, why should she be telling the truth about being William's sister? About being in love with her—if that were true then how could she have been abandoned so easily?

Suddenly she was no longer filled with sorrow but anger, wrath at being spurned and betrayed; hatred welled up inside her.

With malice and intent, Evelyn marched up to the farmhouse to turn in the highwaywoman.

She stood at the door and took a last deep breath before reaching for the knocker.

"Evie!"

Surprised, Evelyn turned to see Bess at the corner of the house, holding a small bag.

"You're up!" she said.

She looked back the way she'd come before stepping forward and grabbing Evelyn by the wrist.

"Come on, we'd better make a run for it."

Evelyn barely had time to ask 'why?' before she was being pulled along across the farmyard back toward the road; she thought Bess might yank her arm from its socket.

"Bess?" was all she managed to say as they ran towards the edge of the farm; her legs, still not recovered from the day before, were in agony as she struggled to keep up the pace the highwaywoman set.

Bess glanced back at the house and her face fell.

Evelyn felt her stomach twist and as she turned to see what Bess was looking at, she saw someone, staggering out of the house.

As he saw them, he called out.

"Johnny, get up, get the dogs!"

The fear forced Evelyn to dig deep within herself and find the stamina she needed to run.

They reached the edge of the farm and Bess pulled her to the right, uphill. They could hear dogs barking; they were gaining on them. Bess dragged her along the road the road towards a break in hedgerow, there was a stile and Bess hurried over.

Tired and panicked Evelyn struggled to lift her legs over the steps.

"Come on, come on!" Bess cried.

Bess pulled her arm and Evelyn tripped over the barrier, falling into Bess' arms. Bess simply pulled her up and they were off again. They ran along the edge of a field next to some woodland. The dogs had taken a moment to pick up their trail but Evelyn turned and saw them at the stile.

Suddenly Bess took a dive into the woods, there was bracken and low lying branches, their progress was slowed as Evelyn's dress was snagged. She cried out as her hair got caught on something and yanked at her head. Bess spun around, her face full of fear and concern she unhooked Evelyn from the tree.

"We have to keep moving," she said.

"I know!" Evelyn cried, insulted that Bess assumed she wanted to get caught on a tree.

The barking was continuous, telling them exactly where the dogs were and Evelyn knew it wouldn't be long before they caught up with them.

The bracken eased off; they sped up, finding it easier to run through the trees. Evelyn felt as though her chest was about to burst but Bess seemed to fly through the woods and know exactly where they were going, she wasn't even concerned when their path was blocked by a six-foot wall.

"What now!?" Evelyn asked panicking and looking around for another path.

Bess tossed the bag she was carrying over the wall and turned to Evelyn.

"Give me a leg up?"

"A leg up?"

"Just do it, Evie!"

Evelyn wasn't even sure what a 'leg up' was. Bess grabbed her hands and pushed them together. They could hear the dogs getting closer. Evelyn leaned against the wall and Bess used her as a ladder to reach up and hoist herself on to the top. She wondered if Bess was just going to disappear and leave her to the dogs.

But she swung her legs over the other side, and then reached her arm down for Evelyn.

"Come on," she said.

"I can't!" she cried; there was nothing for a foothold, the wall was too high, and she started to panic.

The dogs were upon them and Evelyn screamed. She reached up to Bess, who held her tightly with both hands.

"Climb up! Brace your arms against mine and climb up!"

She managed to get off the ground, with her feet placed flat against the wall and her backside sticking out; her skirts hung down and the dogs were leaping to grab hold of her.

"I can't move!" she shouted, looking down at the leaping dogs.

"You have to!"

Bess was using her whole body as a counter balance, but Evelyn could see she was in pain and couldn't pull her any higher.

She managed to shuffle up a few inches and Bess pulled her arms as if she was hoisting a bucket from a well. Finally, she managed to pull her to the top. Evelyn grabbed the wall and her legs flailed out wildly as one of the dogs leapt up, grabbing hold off her foot momentarily. She cried out shaking the dog off and Bess leaned down, grabbing hold of the laces on the back of her bodice, pulling her up onto her stomach. She grappled with the wall and managed to hoist both legs over; she ended up laying uncomfortably on her stomach, looking at the dogs as they seemed to leap higher with every jump.

They knew Johnny wouldn't be far behind, but he hadn't managed to pick up the trail just yet.

"Come on." Bess didn't wait for her, she simply slid off and hit the ground.

Evelyn looked down, she was so sick of running and jumping and falling. For a moment, she wondered if life would be so bad if she just stayed on the wall.

"Come on, Evie!"

She was clutching the wall as her legs dangled, she had a flashback to the moment on the window ledge and wished she could just go back there and never jump out that damned window.

She pushed herself off and landed with a bump on the

ground.

Bess had picked up the bag and pulled out what looked like a chunk of meat, she threw it over and the barking suddenly stopped. It left a ringing in her ears.

"We have to keep moving," Bess said, "and for God's sake keep quiet."

"Where are we?" Evelyn asked, heaving herself off the ground.

"We're on the Harker's' estate."

FIFTEEN

"The Harker's'." Evelyn paused for a moment, before remembering. "Isn't this where you were going for a ball?"

Bess looked at her for a moment, she seemed unwilling to speak.

"Yes," she said eventually.

"Why are we here?" Evelyn was suspicious—she couldn't quite see the advantage of crawling around an estate, but she felt that Bess might be up to something.

"I just thought of it when we were running along the road, I knew we could hide here. Now come on."

Bess was talking in an urgent whisper and Evelyn knew it wouldn't be long before Johnny would catch up with the dogs and realise where they had gone. She wondered if he would be as nimble as Bess in climbing the wall, or if he would simply give up on them.

Bess led her through the dense trees, keeping the wall to their left. Occasionally she would stop and listen, looking carefully around for gamekeepers or a gardener. She knew that they would be seen a mile away with Bess in her bright red dress—they had to do something, they couldn't just keep crawling through the undergrowth.

"Perhaps we could go and explain," she hissed to Bess.

Bess turned and looked at her with confusion.

"Go where and explain what?"

"Up to the house and tell them what's happened, I mean, look at us, they are hardly going to think we're poachers dressed like this."

"And what exactly do we say to them?" Bess said angrily. "Oh, I am terribly sorry to burst in on you during breakfast, Lord and Lady Harker, only my brother is rather angry that I've ruined his plans for kidnap and fraud, oh and I do wish to make my apologies for missing the ball last night, only I had a prior engagement in a barn."

"Well you don't have to say it quite like that…"

"Evelyn, please, I am just as guilty as my brother. There is no reason for them to spare me."

"But if you explain—"

"Shh!" Bess suddenly pressed her finger to Evelyn's lips; she was looking past her into the woods. She held her shoulders and gently moved her behind the trunk of a tree and they hunkered down near its roots.

Evelyn held her breath and closed her eyes, she wanted to ask what it was, if it was a dog or a gamekeeper or a member of the household out for a stroll. But she didn't want to know, she didn't want to have to run again and if she just stayed quiet, if she didn't move, then perhaps it would all just go away.

"It's alright," whispered Bess, finally. "They're gone."

Evelyn breathed out in relief.

"I'm sorry," said Bess suddenly, "I shouldn't have snapped, I just," she sighed, "if you want to go up to the house, perhaps go up to the servants first, and explain. Tell them everything, I'd understand. I can make a dash for it, I would be fine, I've had to look after myself before—"

"No!" Evelyn was horrified at the thought of being on her own again. "You can't leave me! Not now." Evelyn realised she was giving up a chance of walking into safety, into warmth. There would be food, a fire, clothes, and an understanding audience, she could get word to her father, her new friends would look after her. But there would be no Bess.

After last night with her, and thinking she'd lost her this morning, Evelyn couldn't bear the thought of being separated from Bess. It worried her slightly but it also made her feel complete.

Bess smiled and reached forward to stroke Evelyn's cheek.

"In that case," she said quietly, "we're in this together."

They held one another's gaze for a moment before Bess broke the silence.

"We should keep moving," she said.

She helped Evelyn up off the ground and they carefully walked along the edge of the estate.

The birds were still singing their chorus and the air was beginning to warm up, after all the running and jumping and general trauma Evelyn started to calm down and almost felt as though she could be enjoying herself despite her discomfort.

"It's not too far now," said Bess after a few moments. "The gatehouse is just up ahead."

Suddenly she stopped. She was looking straight ahead, staring into the middle distance.

"Is everything alright?" asked Evelyn.

Bess turned and looked behind them; Evelyn turned to look as well but couldn't work out what it was that Bess was staring at.

"I need you to wait here," she said finally.

"Wait here?" Evelyn was aghast, they had just promised to stay together and now Bess was running off.

"I won't be long," she promised, "but I need you to wait here a moment." She handed Evelyn the bag she had been carrying and turned to leave.

"What's in here?"

"Bread, you should have some."

"Where did you get bread from?"

"From back at the farmhouse, before you woke up."

"Is it stolen?"

Bess' look told her it was, but she didn't have time to say anything further. Bess took off at a half-run through the trees, and Evelyn went to sit on the ground with her back to the wall.

She was hungry enough to eat the bread but her conscience wouldn't allow it. There was no excuse for theft, she had been taught that from an early age, and even though she had forgiven Bess her crimes it didn't mean that she was prepared to eat her ill-gotten gains.

She wondered if the past would catch up with them, if by staying with Bess she had now put herself in the position where she was being chased by both criminals and the authorities, perhaps Bess expected her to turn criminal herself, to hold up coaches on the road back to Bristol to pay for their night's rest.

Perhaps this was all part of her plan, an elaborate scheme to plunder her whole estate by gaining her trust. Perhaps William had nothing to do with this at all. Perhaps he was just an innocent caught up in this intrigue.

But then she remembered seeing them together at the inn. She hadn't realised until now how startlingly similar they were in looks: they had those same dark eyes, the same colour hair, and although Bess was frailer and more delicate, they both shared the same features. Bess had to be telling the truth, at least about being Mr Barrington's sister.

Besides it did make some sense—the business transactions, her father's foolish trust, the constant companionship, the sudden proposal and then delay after delay with the wedding. Then she remembered that it had even been William that had suggested the visit to Cambridge, he had persuaded her father to allow her to travel alone.

It all made sense.

Bess had simply been embroiled in her brother's plans, she had no will of her own when it came to the robberies or the fraud—in fact, she'd stepped in to save Evelyn at every possible moment.

As she thought more about it, she slowly started to feel more confident about her decision. She would save Bess, she would make sure that she was safe from the authorities and they would know that she had just been an innocent in all of this.

Even the bread that she taken had been from the farmhouse where Johnny had spent the night, so it was likely that they were criminals as well, and theft from criminals can't really be seen as theft at all.

Without further worry or concern she dipped her hand into the bag and broke off a piece of bread. It wasn't fresh but it didn't matter, she was so hungry she devoured it instantly.

She was deciding how much more she could eat and still leave enough for Bess when she heard a rustle in the trees to her right.

She wondered if a gamekeeper had tracked her down, or if Johnny had followed her and Bess into the estate.

She held her breath, hoping that whoever it was would just walk past without noticing her sitting against the wall.

"Evie!"

She stood, and saw Bess up ahead, creeping through the undergrowth. It took her a moment to realise that she was pulling a horse after her.

"Where did you get that?"

"Shh!" Bess looked behind her. "I think I may have been followed," she whispered.

"You stole a horse!"

"Yes, it's good, isn't it?"

"No, it is not good! You can't steal a horse!"

"Well, it is done, Evelyn. Now we must go, we're in this together, remember?"

"I didn't know that it would involve stealing a horse! Horse theft is a hanging crime."

"They'll hang me for theft, kidnap and highway robbery; they can't hang me more for stealing a horse."

Evelyn opened and closed her mouth. As flawed as Bess' logic was, she couldn't argue with it.

"Look," said Bess, still whispering, "how about we take

this horse now, but when we get back to your estate we write to the Harker's and compensate them for it."

"I don't know…"

"Evelyn, please! Think about this. You're suggesting we walk the whole way to Bristol—that could days, maybe weeks… we would die of starvation before we got close. With my way, we cause someone a minor inconvenience and could be in Bristol by tomorrow, whereupon you can compensate everyone as much as you like."

"But I can't steal a horse."

They heard shouts in the distance; Bess looked at her, pleading.

"I love you Evelyn, I really do (she said it so matter-of-factly, Evelyn was a little taken aback), and I am going to Bristol, and I am going on this horse. Are you coming with me?"

Evelyn struggled, she knew that whoever had chased Bess was getting closer, but she felt the longer she was with Bess, the further she was travelling down the wrong path. She closed her eyes.

"Yes."

Bess let out a sigh of relief, and threw herself up onto the horse, before giving Evelyn a hand. Then, without looking back, they took off at a gallop.

Niamh Murphy

SIXTEEN

The horse sped through the meadow.

Evelyn held on tight to Bess; they didn't seem to be slowing down any time soon. She glanced behind her; she couldn't see anyone in pursuit, but she knew that if they stopped here then they could easily be found, easily be caught up with.

Suddenly the horse leapt over a ditch—she hadn't been paying attention and was nearly thrown. She decided to hold on tighter and just keep her head forward for a while. Bess veered towards the crest of a hill and, as they reached the top, they could see the landscape stretched out before them. The horse cantered down the slope and headed towards a wooded grove.

As soon as they were beyond the trees they slowed to a

trot, and once they were hidden deep inside the wood, Bess said they could dismount.

Evelyn stretched her legs a little before sitting down, while Bess took the horse over to a stream.

She was starting to feel hungry, all she could think about was the bread she'd had earlier; she wished she'd saved a little, wished she'd thought of asking at the house for food. She knew she couldn't have done so without explaining everything and turning in Bess, but she couldn't get the notion out of her mind.

"You should have some water," said Bess, without turning.

Evelyn had never drunk the same water as a horse, but then she had never been on the run from felons before either.

She was going to have to do what was necessary.

Reluctantly she knelt on the ground, a little up-stream from the animal, and cupped her hand, taking in just a little of the water. It was cool and refreshing—it even tasted a little sweet. Before she knew what she was doing she dipped her lips to the water, drinking it up in great gulps. It cured the thirst but didn't touch the hunger.

"We should start moving on," said Bess.

Evelyn hadn't quite recovered from the first bout of riding, but she knew Bess was right; she watched her climb up onto the horse and reluctantly took her place behind her. Bess turned the horse around and they started off at a canter though the woods.

***

They'd been riding all day and finally, as the sun had

started to set, Bess suggested they find a place to camp.

They settled on a clearing, near to a river, there was plenty of dry wood about and Bess could set about making a fire. They had hardly exchanged a word since the Harker's. Bess sat across from Evelyn in the dark and occasionally poked at the fire with a stick.

"Thank you," said Evelyn eventually.

"What for?" Bess asked, looking at her through the fire.

"I wouldn't have been able to ride all day if you hadn't given me that food this morning, and we certainly wouldn't have made it this far without a horse, so even though you stole it, I'm thankful."

"That's alright. I just wish we'd had more than bread."

They fell back into silence and Evelyn felt guilty about having been so angry with her. She was starting to wonder if Bess regretted coming with her, regretted putting herself and her brother in danger by telling her what they'd planned.

She wanted to talk to Bess, to get her to open up, to find out everything about her. She wanted to somehow repair the damage she had caused and try to understand the girl she had run away with.

"How did it all happen?" she asked.

"How did what happen?"

Evelyn tried to think of a tactful way of putting it.

"When you became a…"

"A thief?"

Evelyn looked away: she hadn't intended to be so brutal.

"Yes," she said.

"Well…" Bess sighed; she seemed to be thinking how

best to start the story. "I grew up on a farm, the farm we took you to."

"That house was yours?" Evelyn was surprised; it had seemed such a grand house, and such an old house, as if it hadn't been used for decades. She was surprised that it must only be a few years since it had been lived in and that Bess had grown up as part of a grand family.

"Yes, you stayed in my room. It seemed like a safe place…"

She drifted off, as if remembering.

Evelyn thought back to the room, back to the dolls' house and the powder blue walls; she had wondered at the time what had happened to the little girl that had lived there, why she had left so quickly, where she had gone. It hadn't occurred to her that it was Bess.

"I was happy there, for a while. My mother and father lived there with William and me. I missed him terribly when he went to school—I wanted to go with him." She laughed at the memory. "I had a governess, she was a very prim woman. I don't remember getting on with her particularly well. It wasn't long after my brother went to school that the trouble started. I was too young to understand what was going on, but I would overhear raised voices occasionally, and the servants would whisper in the corridors about my parents. Then my brother came back."

Evelyn waited, and hoped Bess would continue.

"After he came back it was as if something had changed, I found out later that they didn't have the money to keep him there, William was ashamed, and embarrassed of my father. You see, he had started to gamble it away, started to lose it all.'

"We didn't lose the farm in one go. My father sold off bits and pieces to pay his creditors, until there was nothing left. First the servants left, then the animals went, then, piece by piece, the land was sold. It was like a disease, eating away at the farm, eating at my father and quietly, without any of us noticing, it was eating away at my mother as well." She continued to poke the fire, staring into it. When she eventually started to talk again, her voice was slow and measured.

"I was nine, and Billy was about fourteen, when my mother finally disappeared… She just got up one day and left. It was too much for her to cope with. It must have seemed like there was no other way out for her. Billy told me there had been arguments, about money, about the farm, about cards and gambling, and about the nights Pa would come home drunk.'

"At first our father acted as if nothing had happened, as if nothing was different. But it was different. Everything was different. He didn't just go out some nights any more, he went out every night. It was like he had just… sort of… given up. Billy tried to keep the farm going, but Pa owed so much, it was all he could do to keep us fed, and eventually he sold off the last two fields to the Raker's, and we continued to work it at a rent."

"Is that when you decided to … you know…"

"Decided to become a thief?" Bess stared at her through the flames. "No. I stayed at the farm for a few years, worked the fields with the others. Then when I was thirteen my mother called for me, and I moved to London to be with her."

"Well, that must have been a relief, to have her back."

Bess' look told her it wasn't.

"I stayed with her for a while, but it was… difficult. She wasn't always sober; she wasn't easy to be around. Then—I don't know how it happened, a pub brawl or something—my father was killed—"

"I'm sorry..."

Bess shrugged, and continued with her story.

"That was when Billy came to find me. We didn't live with my mother for very long. Billy found it harder to be with her than I did, and one day they argued about something or other and he just packed his bags."

"He left you?"

"We both left."

"And that was when…?"

Bess laughed, bitterly.

"Yes, that was when I started to steal." She looked back into the fire and paused for a moment before continuing.

"At first, we both just took whatever we could get, we knew it was a risk… I knew a boy, just a boy, who was hanged for stealing a watch… a watch!" Bess shook her head, as if still reeling from the injustice. "Billy wanted more than that, he said we deserved more, our grandfather had been titled, and Billy had been to a good school, known good people, tasted culture, we'd just…"

"Fallen on hard times?" she said, repeating the expression she'd heard so often before when people spoke of the misfortune of others, but she'd never fully comprehended the devastation that mild phrase could imply.

"Exactly. We'd fallen on hard times, and Billy said he could get us back to the top, back to where we deserved to be, he said he could get us both married to rich landowners, and our children would never have to go through what we'd been through, they'd never have to know what it was like to break your back in the fields at harvest time, or scrub a man's shoes for a farthing, or hear their mother through the walls earning her keep... he said I would never have to go through that, he promised me that I would never have to stoop as low as our mother had."

Bess looked up, and Evelyn saw fear, and pleading in her eyes.

"Please don't turn him in, Evie."

Evelyn was silent—she didn't want to promise anything, she wanted to see justice done, to know that her father would see justice done. She couldn't promise to protect a thief, a fraudster, a kidnapper. But then again, she was already protecting Bess.

"Please don't," Bess repeated. "He only did all of this for me, he only did what he thought was right to get us out of this, to make sure we'd be safe. I can't see him hang... I can't."

"I won't," she said. "I won't hand him in. I promise." The moment the words were out of her mouth she regretted them, she hoped that she would never have to live by that promise, but the relief on Bess' face was clear. She moved around the fire to sit next to her, and slid her fingers between Evelyn's.

"Thank you," she whispered.

Evelyn breathed deeply, staring into the flames, and holding Bess' hand. She had so much to take in.

She was still hungry and that shocked her—she had never been so hungry for so long before.

She thought of Bess, Bess the nine-year-old, Bess the

fourteen-year-old. How different had she been? What had she gone through when she had been forced on to the streets? How long had she gone hungry for before she had decided to steal from someone for the first time?

How could that be so wrong? How can it be wrong for a child to take the food it needs to survive?

She started to imagine the boy that had stolen the watch, the boy that was hung for the sake of a few guineas, if that. She wondered how much life was worth. How much was her life worth? How much was Bess' life worth?

She held Bess closer at the thought of losing her, at the thought of her having been so close to being lost forever, and suddenly she was glad. She was glad that Bess had been a thief, glad that she had been clever enough not to get caught and brave enough to do it in the first place. If she hadn't, if she had died on the streets as a child, then Evelyn wouldn't have her here now, she wouldn't be sitting with her in the woods, away from everyone, away from the world, just her and her highwaywoman.

She looked up at Bess, at her beautiful profile as she stared into the fire.

Evelyn reached up and pulled Bess's chin toward her own, and Bess melted into her as they kissed.

SEVENTEEN

Evelyn felt the soft warmth of the sun on her face; she opened her eyes, looking around and hoping to see Bess lying next to her.

But the space beside her was bare.

She sat up. The fire had died and, despite the early morning sun, she felt cold. She started to poke the embers with a stick to get it going again, to try to get warmth back into her aching bones. She didn't want to start panicking about Bess; she didn't want to think ill of her just yet. She would wait a while at least.

She rubbed her sore neck and caught her hand on her necklace. She opened it carefully, remembering. Remembering the moment he had given it to her, how she had felt, the world she had known. So much had changed since then.

Then she remembered Bess, how she had known her name, how she must have known exactly who she was after reading the locket. She laughed bitterly as she realised that must have been the only reason William had given it to her, so her captors would know who to follow and pick off at the right moment.

She yanked it from her neck and threw it off into the undergrowth, sick of the memory, then lay back against the tree and waited.

It wasn't long before she heard the distant hooves of a horse. She stayed still, knowing that she was well hidden; she would only be spotted by someone that knew where she was. As the hooves came closer, she glanced behind her through the trees. It was Bess. She cantered over and slid off the horse. She was holding a small sack—Evelyn knew it would be stolen—and hoped it would be food. Her stomach was screaming out for sustenance.

"I'm glad you're awake," said Bess as she sat next to her."I wasn't sure if I should go and get any food, I know you don't agree with…"

"I know," said Evelyn. She was finally starting to understand, to fully appreciate, the position someone would be in when they contemplated stealing from others. To be willing to risk the noose to steal is much easier when you are starving.

She took the bag from Bess and looked inside. There was bread and cheese, and it looked like there was a pie in there as well, but she decided to save that for later.

As she started to eat what was probably one of the best meals of her life, she made a promise to herself: never to judge someone so harshly again, and to make far more donations to the alms-houses. In fact, she should build an alms-house, so no one would ever have to steal food just to stay alive.

"How much farther do you think it?" she asked, realising she had no idea where they were. She could have been taken a hundred miles in the wrong direction and she wouldn't know. She was completely relying on Bess and her knowledge of the country.

"I think it's about another day's ride," she said. "If we ride hard we could make it by tonight, but I don't know how hard we can ride the horse with two people on her."

"We should get moving then," said Evelyn, feeling satisfied after the food and eager to finally get home.

***

By late afternoon they were hot and sweaty. The early autumn sun beat down on their backs. They'd hardly rested all day and Evelyn was starting to feel drowsy—she was thinking about the pie she'd seen in the bag and was hoping that they could rest and eat. She was no longer desperate to get home, she just wanted to stop.

They were following a river, looking for an easy place to cross. The water was slow running, but it was deep and rocky. It opened in to a cool clear pool, the light danced on the surface and she could see the bottom through the clear water.

She took advantage of the opportunity and suggested they stop and have a rest for a while.

"We could just stop here for the night," Bess said.

"The night?" Evelyn couldn't believe her good luck.

"We will have to stop to rest at some point, we won't

make it to Bristol today so we may as well get a good night's rest and then continue on in the morning."

"That sounds good," said Evelyn, sliding off the horse, relieved that it would be hours before she would have to get back on.

Bess got started on a fire. It was still warm but she said they would be glad for it when they got out of the water, and Evelyn thought now would be an ideal opportunity to give some attention to her clothes. She took off her dress and could take out some of the worst of the mud—Bess did the same with hers—and they left them to dry by the fire.

Evelyn was slightly nervous about jumping in the river: she thought they could be seen by passing strangers. But Bess had no such reservations: she completely stripped and leapt in, diving underneath. Evelyn was reminded of the dream she'd had of drowning while the mermaid Bess had swum around her. She threw the images from her mind and cast off her underclothes, delicately stepping into the pool. She was tired of dark thoughts and simply wanted to celebrate her freedom.

The water was cool and crisp. It felt like ice against her hot skin, invigorating her, waking her up and refreshing her.

"It's beautiful, isn't it?" she said.

Bess laughed. It was good to hear her laugh—it seemed as though she'd hardly laughed since they first met. It felt reassuring and washed away the stress and the tension she had felt over the last few days; she had been worried for her life, for her safety, for her wealth and her father, she had been kidnapped, escaped, been chased, been betrayed, and had become a thief, all within a few hours of one another. She needed space to be herself again.

To let everything wash away from her.

It felt as though the water was not just purifying her body but it was purging her soul as well.

Bess swam towards and kissed her softly on the lips. She held on to her and their warm bodies pressed against one another in the cool water.

"You're shivering!" said Bess.

"I think I'm cold," she said, suddenly laughing through chattering teeth, allowing her anxiety to fall away. Bess grinned and they clambered out of the pool.

They sat by the fire in their underclothes and Bess split the pie in half. Evelyn was delighted to have the food and finally she lay down, feeling clean, dry, warm and fed.

The sun started to ease its way lower in the sky, and Evelyn looked up at the stars slowly appearing, one after the other, as Bess cuddled up to her.

"I used to love looking up at the stars as a child," Bess whispered.

"Tell me more about what it was like growing up." Evelyn wanted to know everything.

"A lot of it was good," she said after a while. "But a lot of it was hard. Even before my mother left, my father had always been hard. He was a disciplinarian, and his punishments were severe…"

Evelyn held Bess tightly. She wrapped herself around her as if she could somehow protect her from the memory. She wanted to keep her safe and away from everything.

"I won't let anyone hurt you again."

Bess laughed, and stroked Evelyn's head.

"I know."

"I mean it!" said Evelyn, sitting up. "You can live with

me. You'll be my companion, my father will agree, he knows I have been lonely since I moved to Bristol."

"But what about everything that's happened? Will he be so welcoming when he finds out what I have done?"

"We'll sort that out, we'll explain, he will understand what has happened, he'll forgive you, once he understands the way I do then he will know that you aren't a criminal."

She snuggled up to Bess and started to let the exhaustion of the day wash over her.

"You'll live at my house," said Evelyn sleepily. "It's an old house, Tudor, I think; it's beautiful, especially in the summer. The gardens are lush and there are apple trees, there is a wood at the bottom of the garden as well, and there is a path lined with trees. Sometimes it feels as if all the trees are standing to attention as you walk past, and you can imagine yourself to be Titania, Queen of the woods."

Bess almost snorted with laughter.

"Well you don't have to do that, but you can walk all through the grove, and there is a kitchen garden as well—I think it is as old as the house. It has a great wall running all the way around it, and all along the walls are fruit trees; there are plums and quinces and lines of raspberry bushes. But that garden is different to the walled garden, which has a statue of Poseidon in it, the one with the trident."

"Why does it have a statue of Poseidon?" Bess was almost asleep; her eyes were closed and her voice was sleepy.

"I don't know, something to do with the harbour I think."

She looked at Bess, her soft white skin against her dark hair. She was beautiful. Evelyn could hardly believe that someone so beautiful, so perfect, could be with her. She leaned forward and kissed her softly on the cheek, before laying back and looking back up the sky.

The sky was completely black and the stars were like a blanket of diamonds, with hardly a cloud to obscure the view.

'It's going to be alright,' she thought to herself. 'Everything is going to be alright.'

***

It was a few hours after sunrise when they rode over the peak of a hill and she saw it in the distance, between the trees, a glimpse of home.

"There it is!" she yelled, pointing.

"I see it," Bess replied, as she kicked the horse into a gallop. Evelyn held on tightly as they hurtled across the meadow towards home.

Their pace steadied as they came to the road and they cantered along the country lane.

Evelyn smiled as she thought of seeing her father's face, of eating decent food, a decent bed, clean clothes, and she squeezed Bess slightly in excitement. As they turned the corner, Abberton Hall came into view.

Evelyn let out a breath she felt she'd been holding since the moment she'd left. She loved the sight of her house and garden; she expected to see the dogs running out to greet them any moment as they cantered towards it.

Bess stopped the horse just outside the front door; she paused for a moment taking in the full spectacle before slipping off and turning to help Evelyn.

As Evelyn touched the ground, the front door opened,

she looked up expecting to see Garret, a look of startled delight across his usually composed countenance. But her face fell as she saw a musket. Bess caught her eye and spun round to see Charlie standing in the doorway. He swung the musket up to point directly at them.

"You took your time."

EIGHTEEN

"Charlie!" Bess took a small step forward. "What are you doing here?"

He smiled but didn't lower the musket.

"We didn't have much choice, Bessie, someone insisted on keeping our hostage untied, and they got away."

"How did you get here so quickly?"

She seemed genuinely surprised and yet Evelyn started to wonder. Had she been expecting them? Had this been arranged? Just whose side was this girl on? Evelyn instinctively took a step back from her.

"We rode," he replied. "What did you do? Stop for naps and picnics?" He laughed at his own joke and headed towards them, musket in hand.

Evelyn struggled to read Bess' expression. She smiled

161

at Charlie's joke, but was it a forced smile or was it genuine? She couldn't tell, she couldn't read Bess' mind and she was starting to wonder if she knew her at all.

"Did you know they would be here?" she hissed.

She knew it was probably stupid to ask but she needed to know, she needed some reassurance from somewhere that this wasn't all part of the plan, that she hadn't just been betrayed again.

Bess turned to look at her. Charlie was just a few feet away and Evelyn noticed that he was holding the musket aimed squarely at her, not Bess.

"You still don't trust me, do you?" Bess asked. Those dark eyes looked at her with pleading, the same pleading she'd seen in her eyes before when trying to convince her, trying to explain.

Evelyn opened her mouth but couldn't provide a response. She didn't know what to say, she felt herself being drawn into those eyes again she looked away. She couldn't get taken in again, not now, not when it was so clear that, after everything that had happened, Bess was still one of them.

"Come on! Stop your natter and get inside!" Charlie waved the musket. Bess turned and walked up to the house. Evelyn reluctantly followed.

Charlie giggled as they passed.

"What have you two been up to?" he asked, shaking his head. "William is going to be delighted to see you."

Evelyn's stomach turned. William. She hadn't seen him since the inn, since she'd walked in on him and Bess. She didn't know how he would react when he saw her, if he knew what she had been told, or how much of it was the truth. She knew from the way they looked so similar that

Bess must have been telling the truth about being his sister, and by the way Charlie was acting now it was utterly clear that William was, and probably always had been, a part of the gang.

She desperately wanted to know what they were doing at her house, how they had got inside. She wondered if they had the servants all lined up in one of the rooms, under armed guard, just as she had been that night of the stage coach robbery.

Suddenly she thought about her father and whether he was safe or not. She wondered just how much he now knew about what had happened to her and whether he knew about all the money he had lost through trusting William. She felt for him, not just for the danger he was in, but also for the humiliation he must be facing.

Charlie marched them through the house and up towards her father's study; Bess hesitated outside the door.

"Go on in," he said.

She glanced back at Evelyn; she seemed a little nervous but pushed open the door and stepped inside. Charlie pushed Evelyn in the back with the musket and she followed Bess through the open door.

Evelyn gasped as she saw her father sitting on the chaise longue, his hands together in his lap. He looked up as she entered; there was a look of shock on his face and then sadness, defeat, as if the last ounce of hope had vanished the moment she entered.

He lowered his head and was like a man lost.

She hadn't seen him like that since the day her mother died, but even then, when he'd looked at her he had been hopeful. Today, he was defeated.

Johnny stood guard next to him, leaning against the

bookcases, his musket under his arm. He smiled as he looked at Evelyn. It sent a chill through her as she remembered the glee on his face that first time he had whacked her across the head. Bess had led her to him that time as well.

William stood at the desk with his back to them, hastily rifling through papers. He had removed his jacket and was wearing a long-tailored waistcoat and shirt, his powdered wig perfectly coiffed.

Jim leaned on the desk next to him and nudged him as he saw Evelyn enter. William turned and looked at them in surprise, the frustration slid from his face and he laughed in delight, striding forward.

"I knew you'd find your way here eventually!"

He grabbed hold of Bess, pulling her toward him into a swift embrace, then held her by the arms, looking at her and laughing again.

"How did you find her?" he asked, ignoring Evelyn completely.

"She was in the Raker's barn," Bess replied. She glanced briefly at Evelyn but turned back to her brother's gaze. Evelyn looked away from the scene—it made her feel sick to see Bess so quickly part of the gang again.

"And how did you know we would come here?"

"Well I didn't really... I ... took a chance."

Evelyn closed her eyes. So, Bess had led her here, led her like a lamb to the slaughter, and she had followed. Followed with trust and excitement, she had even been given the choice to turn her in and had refused. She was so stupid, so utterly stupid, to have trusted a thief and a villain.

Bess was rotten to the core and she had been taken in

completely.

"You're like a homing pigeon," laughed William, "and did you find out how she escaped in the first place?" His tone had changed from inquisitive to interrogative.

"She… I don't know… I left Charlie in charge of her."

"Hey!" Said Charlie stepping forward, but the word was hardly out of his mouth before William had punched him in the head.

Evelyn jumped, there had been an audible crack and she watched in horror as Charlie fell, limply, to the floor. She stared at him in shock and felt herself become a little shaky, she had never seen anyone fall in such a way before, and she had never seen anyone lash out so violently.

She looked at William, she remembered how they had walked together in the gardens, how he had seemed such a good friend—she would never have believed him so capable of violence. But then she looked across at his sister and realised that they were both equally efficient at concealing their true character.

Relieved of his frustration, William straightened his waistcoat and turned back to Bess.

"At least I can rely on you." He smiled and put his hand on Bess' arm before finally turning and facing Evelyn.

He stared at her for a long hard moment, she stared back, her heart was pounding in her chest, she had no idea what he was about to do, no idea what he was capable of. She wondered if she would be next, if he would just attack her for having escaped, for having ruined his plans.

"I would very much appreciate it if you would take a seat with your father, Miss Thackeray." Evelyn was stunned: his tone and manner had been completely altered.

For a moment, he was as if nothing had changed, as if they were back on their winter walks and he was simply making a polite request of his fiancée. She couldn't understand how anyone could flip between two strikingly different characters so quickly,

"NOW!" he barked.

She gasped. Startled and shaking, she quickly crossed the room and sat down next to her father. She didn't understand how William could keep his violent demons concealed so effectively, and she wondered just what Bess had hidden beneath that beautiful and innocent exterior.

She looked at her father. He was pale and tired. He seemed so old and frail; she was frightened for him. She placed a hand over his and mustered a smile.

"I'm sorry, Evelyn," he whispered. "So, sorry, so very, very sorry."

He mumbled for a few moments more, but he didn't look up from ground.

She was filled with guilt, he had only wanted the best for her: some good investments, a decent husband, someone to help run the estate when he was gone. He had not intended any of this and he was carrying the guilt for the whole debacle.

Yet it was her fault, she had willingly stepped out of the carriage into Bess' arms. She had been ready to throw him over, throw all his hard work away, leave the estate and leave him alone in his dotage in order to run away with a double-crossing highwaywoman. It was her fault, the whole mess was her fault, her madness over a girl. A girl that had now betrayed them all.

She closed her eyes, hoping that somehow it would all go away.

"Well!" started William, with a deep grin of satisfaction across his face. He stood proudly in the centre of the study like a teacher addressing a room of schoolboys.

"This makes everything much simpler, doesn't it?" He laughed, and looked over at Evelyn's father. "Now, Mr Thackeray, I don't believe you've had the pleasure of meeting my sister." He pulled Bess forward by the arm. "Miss Elizabeth Barrington, Bessie to her friends, isn't that right, Bessie?"

She nodded slowly, her face passive and unreadable. Evelyn's father stared at the ground, and she wasn't sure if he was even aware of what was going on.

"Now, my dear Mr Thackeray, I do believe you owe a debt of gratitude to my sister here, on account of her bringing your daughter safely back to you, across hills and valleys, and no doubt through terrible danger, isn't that right Bessie?" He smiled at her and proudly patted her on the back.

Evelyn's father slowly looked up.

"I'm sorry," he said, to no one in particular, his whisper was barely audible.

"What did he say?" asked William, striding toward the old man.

"He said 'thank you'," Evelyn said quickly.

She looked at Bess, at the woman who had brought her here, who had lied from the beginning, had snatched her from the carriage and thrown her to the lions. She had jumped sides whenever it was convenient to her and now she was simply showing her true form.

She had lied and cheated and Evelyn had believed her, had forgiven her for her villainy and even thought they might have a future together. She was disgusted by her.

She hated her; she wanted to hurt her, to see her pay for what she had done.

"Thank you," she repeated looking Bess straight in the eyes, and summoning all the venom she could muster.

But Bess looked away.

William stood over her father, as if trying to provoke further fear, further subjugation, but her father didn't move, didn't react. William stepped away, unsatisfied at the result of his game.

He walked toward Jim, still leaning on the desk, a look of mild amusement on his face.

"Go and fetch the parson, would you?"

Jim nodded and stood to leave, but stopped when William clicked his fingers, he clicked again and held out his hand. Jim seemed to understand, and pulled a pistol out of his coat, handing it to William, before leaving the drawing room, stepping over Charlie as he went.

William turned to face Evelyn and her father as he inspected the pistol, ensuring it was loaded and ready to fire.

"Now," said William, looking up at Evelyn, "I do believe that you and I, Miss Thackeray, have an engagement to keep."

NINETEEN

She'd been taken to her room and made to clean up and change while Johnny had waited outside. She had considered leaping out the window, but it had only been a fleeting thought. She couldn't face going through that horror again, and her father was still being held at gunpoint in the study—she couldn't risk causing him harm, or at least no more harm than she had caused him already. Once ready, she had been led downstairs to join the others.

It seemed unreal for her to be sitting in the drawing room having tea served by the maid. It was only at that point she realised none of the servants were aware of what was going on, they simply believed that William was on a visit with associates of his. She had tried to alert the maid, to somehow warn her, explain the situation so that they could send a boy down to the village. They could send up a hue and cry that would force every man with in ten miles to drop everything and come and stop this madness. But Johnny had been watching her like a hawk and she noticed that as the maid walked around the room, politely serving the tea to a gang of vagabonds, he kept the woman in his direct line of fire. Evelyn was sure that the moment she moved, mentioned anything, or did anything that could be seen as a warning, he would simply shoot the maid dead. She couldn't take the risk, and she couldn't keep the maid in danger. She knew she would have to send her away, losing her only opportunity to warn the servants.

"That'll be all, Jones," she said, doing her best to keep her voice level.

She noticed that William looked over as she said it: he was just as keen to make sure that she didn't let on to her situation. But the maid was oblivious; she curtseyed politely and left the room, taking with her Evelyn's last hope.

William seemed satisfied, and he turned back to the parson, seated in the corner of the room. He was a little man, only a touch older than Evelyn herself, and although she had always thought him a genial young fellow, she had never known him to be particularly bright.

He was flustered and taken aback at William's request. She could see he was uncomfortable but at the same time she knew he wouldn't refuse. She knew he was both too intimidated and in awe of William to refuse him any request, and she could tell that, although William was becoming frustrated, he was able to keep calm and gently press the parson into agreeing.

"But I happen to know for certain that the church will be free this Saturday," he was saying in his reedy little voice, which had never been suited to giving sermons. "That should give you ample time to apply for a licence and perhaps for Miss Thackeray to obtain a dress for the occasion?"

He didn't hide his disapproval of her outfit. It was her Sunday best, but it was hardly suited to a wedding, especially not her own. There was also the fact that she hadn't been allowed the help of her lady's maid, so although she had done her utmost not to raise suspicion, she knew that she looked far from her finest.

William nodded to the parson and gave him a dazzling smile, the same smile that had always seemed so warm to Evelyn when they had walked in the gardens, and the same smile that she had seen spread across Bess' face many times over the past few days.

She glanced over at the highwaywoman. She wasn't paying attention to the conversation in the room—she too had been made to tidy herself up—and was now standing at the window looking out over the lawn, completely lost in thought. Evelyn felt the anger rising in her once again, the memories of how they had been together, of how she had been so foolishly taken in. She felt sick with anger and looked away, forcing herself to stare at the cup of tea becoming cold in her hands.

"I would prefer a church wedding, of course," William continued, the lies dripping off his tongue. "However, I shall be leaving the country on business tomorrow, and won't be returning for several months. I fear that leaving the wedding any longer will cause," William dropped his voice and leaned towards the Parson conspiratorially, "a scandal."

The Parson's eyes widened in comprehension and surprise.

"Oh, I, erm…"

He glanced across the room at Evelyn, sitting limply in her chair. She held his gaze for a moment but dropped her eyes. She knew that the moment this hideous affair was over he would go scurrying back to his young wife and reveal this exciting gossip to her and, before the day was out, every man woman and child in the village, and probably then next village over, would be talking about the 'scandal' the young Miss Thackeray had been embroiled in.

She looked away and sighed. What the parson, or anyone else, thought of her really didn't matter anymore. She no longer had the energy to care about her reputation. For today, all she could think about was trying to keep herself and her father out of harm's way for as long as possible.

"I understand," replied the Parson, putting on his most diplomatic and understanding tone. "Since Miss Thackeray is a resident of this parish, then I have full dispensation to complete the wedding immediately."

William smiled broadly and held out his hand.

"Thank you," he said as they shook hands. "Thank you very much."

"Would you like the wedding in here, though it is a lovely day outside?"

"Ah yes!" said William, standing. "It is a beautiful day. How about we all move on to the lawn?" He looked around the room as if expecting a cheer, but Evelyn merely stared blankly back and her father didn't react at all. William took no notice and strode out of the room, quickly followed by the overexcited parson.

"You 'eard him." Johnny stood over Evelyn, his musket under his coat. She stood obediently, and taking her father's hand, they followed the others out into the garden.

The parson and William were standing on the edge of the garden discussing the best place. William seemed to consider for a moment, before pointing to the tree lined avenue, and together they strode off towards it, Johnny forcing Evelyn and her father to follow. Evelyn glanced back as Bess and Jim came out of the front door. It was a far cry from the wedding party that Evelyn had imagined for herself.

As they gathered under the elm trees William took Evelyn's hand. Her father stood next to her, in the shadow of Johnny and his concealed musket, while Bess took her place beside William. Evelyn was all too aware that half the wedding party had guns.

She looked to the ground as the parson began to drone out a speech. She felt empty inside, but as she thought of Bess she felt angry, betrayed—she wanted to hurt her as much as she had been hurt.

But then as she thought of the guns, she was too scared to move, not so much for her, but for her father, her father, who felt so guilty, who had taken the whole burden of this affair on his own shoulders. She knew he felt as though he'd failed, she wanted to tell him that he hadn't. This was her fault. She had been the one whose stupidity and selfishness had got them both to this place.

Then she thought of William.

She didn't know what to think of William, she remembered his face as he had given her the locket; he had seemed so loving, so open, so full of warmth. She had been willing in that moment to spend the rest of her life with him. As she stood there in the sunshine she realised that was still going to happen.

"Miss Thackeray?"

She looked up at the parson.

"Do you take this man?" he repeated.

She looked at William, she didn't know what she was doing, she didn't feel as though it was real, she didn't know what would happen if she went through with the wedding and she didn't know what would happen if she didn't. She thought of their life together, of what might happen.

She wondered if he would demand his marital rights, or simply take all their money and leave. She was horrified at the thought that he may even live with them, keeping them prisoners in their own house, or perhaps he would simply send them away somewhere.

William smiled at her, clamping his hand around hers, slowly getting tighter. She winced in pain and turned back to the parson.

"I do," she said.

Then it was over.

William was thanking the parson emphatically and even inviting him over for dinner, before walking him back around to the front of the house.

Evelyn just stood, in shock in the middle of the path. She felt as though she were in a dream, in another world, a nightmare where, any moment now, she could wake up and none of this would be real. There would be no William, no highwaymen, and no Bess, just her and her father and her quiet afternoons with books. Back to boredom and the safe quiet world she had lived in before.

She just wanted it to end and she felt ready to accept whatever fate William had for her, just as long as it was all over quickly.

She watched William eagerly waving off the parson and then he turned back and marched towards the little wedding party. She was sure she saw a spring in his step.

"Well, you have what you wanted," said Evelyn weakly as he reached their little group.

"Not quite, Mrs Barrington, not quite," said William with a grin.

Her stomach turned as she heard him use the name.

"Mr Thackeray," he continued, "I believe we have some papers to sign, now that you intend to retire and hand your estate to your daughter and your new son-in-law."

"Oh…" Mr Thackeray looked up, he looked confused and tired. Evelyn could see fear in his eyes.

"I… I can't do that," he said.

William was aghast. Evelyn couldn't believe her father would be so foolish as try last minute heroics. It wasn't worth his life to refuse.

"And why not?" said William. His cheery demeanour had gone.

Mr Thackeray looked at Evelyn and then to William. She couldn't begin to imagine what he was trying to do.

"There are the legalities," he said. There was a pleading in his voice, and Evelyn realised he was telling the truth. "The legal framework is in place, Evie—Evelyn cannot take on the estate until she is thirty, my lawyers simply wouldn't have it… it's unheard of."

William roared in frustration, making Evelyn jump.

"You foolish old man!" he shouted, moving towards

her father. "You said nothing of this! Why did you say nothing of this?"

"I... I... you didn't ask!" He was backing away, clearly terrified of the enraged William.

"And what am I supposed to do now?" he asked, as if expecting a reply. "Do you know how many debtors are on my back? Do you have any idea? This suit! That dress!" He pointed to Bess. "These men are waiting to be paid for their work!"

Johnny nodded slowly and smiled. He seemed to be enjoying the scene. William rubbed his temples in frustration.

"And what happens if you die?" he said calmly, looking up at Mr Thackeray.

"Ah..." Her father said, stepping back slowly. "That would be a different matter..."

"I thought so," said William, as he pulled the pistol from his coat.

Evelyn gasped. It was over!

After everything she had been though he was going to kill her father anyway. She hadn't allowed herself to believe that he would be capable, that he would actually be able to commit murder. To look into the eyes of a man he knew, a man he had at least pretended to like—they'd eaten dinner together, shared jokes, talked long in to the night—she hadn't been prepared to believe that he could do it.

William pulled back the flintlock on the pistol.

"I am sorry, sir, but it looks as though you are going to have a hunting accident..."

TWENTY

"NO! William! Put the gun down!"

Suddenly Bess leapt in front of Mr Thackeray.

Evelyn held her father's hand, she could feel him shaking as Bess stood between them and William's gun. Evelyn couldn't quite believe what was happening, she couldn't believe that Bess was saving her father. She wasn't sure if this was somehow part of the ruse, but she knew that didn't make sense. She couldn't believe she was wrong about Bess' betrayal, perhaps it was simply that her conscience wouldn't allow her to watch her brother kill.

"Get out of the way!" William yelled. "You know this has to be done."

"No, Bill, there has to be another way."

"Don't go soft on me now Bess, there is no other way,

we are all in this together, remember?"

"Please, Billy, just put the gun down."

Evelyn wasn't sure from the look on William's face which way this was going to play out. A moment ago, she would have gladly seen Bess take her father's place, but now that she had stepped in front of them, now that Bess was standing in front of the gun, Evelyn was worried for her. Although she wanted to see her safe, she also had to think of her father, she knew he was still in danger, she knew William wouldn't hesitate to kill him, she knew, with absolute certainty, that it was up to her to get him out of there.

"We agreed," William said. "We agreed from the very beginning, that if any one of us betrayed the others, then we would seek vengeance. From where I'm standing, Bess, you are betraying us all. I will do what I have to do whether you move or not."

Evelyn looked to her father. She realised the shot could easily pass through Bess and she would lose everything in one instant. Carefully, slowly, without any sudden movements she stood in front of her father, and pushed him back.

"You're not a murderer, Billy, don't change that. You've got what we came for. This needs to end now."

"You know nothing! You stupid, stupid girl!"

The anger was beginning to rise in his voice and Evelyn could see his cheeks flaring red. She knew he wasn't going to back down. If she was going to do anything, she needed to do it quickly.

She glanced at the highwaymen, Johnny and Jim, either side of Bess and William, watching the situation with intensity, neither one sure what the outcome would be.

Their focus was on the others—they had taken their eyes off Evelyn and her father.

"We have to run," she whispered over her shoulder, as loud as she dare, trying to catch her father's attention.

He looked at her, startled.

Keeping her eyes forward, she nudged her father back.

"Through the trees," she hissed, "to the walled garden."

"William, please," Bess was saying, and Evelyn tentatively inched backwards.

"At this range I'll kill you all with one shot!"

"You can't do it, Billy, not me, not after everything we've been through together!"

Evelyn squeezed her father's hand. For a moment, she was torn. She didn't want to stay, she couldn't stay. She needed to do what she could to get her father as far away as possible, as quickly as possible. She had seconds, if that, and she knew that the moment she made her move, they would be after her. They might even shoot them down, but at least it would give them a fighting chance.

Yet she didn't want to go, she didn't want to tear herself away from Bess and leave her at their mercy. She didn't know what would happen, she wasn't sure any more, she wasn't sure of anything. But she had to do something.

"Bessie, goddammit! Get out of the way!" William was filled with rage.

It was now or never. Evelyn turned and ran.

She pulled her father along behind her and they slipped off the path between two elm trees. Shouting broke out almost instantly behind her, but it had taken them a few seconds to realise what had happened. It was all the time she needed to get to the walled garden and push on the gates. She thanked God they were open. She pulled her father through after her, and behind the wall.

"I don't know if I can do this." He was out of breath already, the alarm, the anxiety, the sudden rush across the lawn, had all gotten to him.

But she didn't have time to pander to his needs; she ignored his pleas and continued to run, around the pond, to the other side of the garden and through the gate. She didn't know how close behind they were, she just gripped her father's hand and kept running.

She pulled him along the path behind her, as they ran uphill towards the kitchen garden. Once there she could send him into the house, just as soon as she got through the entrance to the kitchen garden. It was just a few paces away.

She couldn't resist the urge to look behind her. Her father was red faced and frightened, he was puffing along behind her. She could see he was in pain, could see that this was no good for him. In the distance, she spotted a flash of black—the long coat of a highwayman outspread as he chased them up the path.

Her chest twisted in fear, but the panic urged her forward and she rushed past the wall into the kitchen garden.

She let go of her father and scanned the area, desperately looking for something, anything, to defend herself with. There was a wheelbarrow, a bucket, the compost heap and there, next to the compost, was a shovel.

She grabbed it and turned back to the entrance. She barely had time to think about what she was doing—as Jim came rushing in to the garden, she swung the shovel. He didn't even have a chance to see what was coming: it whacked into his face and he dropped into a heap on the ground before them.

"Evelyn! I…" Her father was struggling to think of an appropriate response to the situation. She knew he was somewhere between praise and a reprimand, but she didn't have time to dwell on what she had done, or what anyone would think of it. She had another one to deal with, somewhere.

"Get to the house, father! Get Garret, tell him what's happening!"

Mr Thackeray hesitated, looking at her in shock and alarm as she stood there wildly gesturing with the shovel.

"Go!" she shouted.

Still confused, he turned and hurried off towards the house. She just hoped he would be safe, hoped he would be able to explain, and that the servants would take him seriously and wouldn't assume that he'd finally gone completely mad.

She had to find Johnny. She had to find him before he found her, or worse, before he found her father. She knew that he would be delighted to get the excuse to kill something—she didn't suppose he knew the difference between a man or a beast. She would have to make sure that she was prepared.

Her heart was pounding at the thought of what she was about to do, but she took a deep breath, and grabbed the pistol from the motionless body of Jim as he lay spread-eagled on the ground.

She peered around the edge of the wall, looking out on to the lawn she had just crossed.

Johnny was there.

He was running across the lawn up to the house, as though intending to head them off. She knew he would find her father, and she knew what he would do to him when he found him. She had barely a second; she needed to get his attention. She could fire at him but she would never hit him at this distance.

She screamed.

Immediately Johnny stopped and looked over to her. She wasn't sure from this distance, but she had a feeling that he smiled when he saw her, and immediately he started heading towards her. She had to run, and she couldn't let him get to the house—she had to lead him away, she had to make him follow her and she had to make damned sure he didn't catch her.

For a few seconds, she stood rooted to the spot, unable to move, frozen, in fear of the black coated apparition of evil that was rushing towards her. She wanted to aim the gun, but her arm wouldn't move.

A sudden shot rang out.

Johnny stopped and looked over to the elm trees. It was enough to bring her to her senses, she ran out of the garden and down the lawn, towards the wood.

She didn't know where she was heading. All she could think was that she had to run quickly. She had to run faster than Johnny and she had to keep him running until her father was safe. But she didn't know how long that would be. She didn't know if she could keep running for that long and she didn't know if he would catch up with her.

She swerved in and out of trees, ignoring the pathways and just hoping Johnny would blindly follow her zigzagging path. Perhaps he would lose her, perhaps he would trip, anything to give her the advantage.

She heard another shot.

She stumbled and fell to the ground, dropping the pistol in the leaves. Panicking, she scrabbled around in the dirt for it. She couldn't see it. She noticed blood on her dress. She stared at it and as the realisation crept in, so did the pain.

Grape shot had torn into her left arm, and the small pellets had dug into her flesh. Johnny must have fired a pot shot into the woods. It had so nearly missed her, but not quite.

She heard a roar behind her, and she turned. He was running towards her, his musket raised above his head like a battle axe. She screamed, and in a panic, she threw handfuls of dirt and leaves at his face. He roared out in pain, flailing his musket blindly.

She scrabbled to her feet. As she did so she saw the pistol. She grabbed it and started to run again.

But Johnny slammed her across the back with his musket. She yelped in pain, staggering to the floor. But she didn't let herself fall. She was on her feet and started forward, forcing herself to run.

She caught a glimpse of the gardener's shed in the distance through the trees. She headed towards it. Maybe she could be safe in there, maybe she could shut him out and hide, distract him long enough for her father to send someone to rescue her.

As she veered towards it, she caught another blow to the back. Johnny slammed the musket against her shoulder and she dropped to her knees.

The shed was still in her sights. She tried to scrabble up, tried to stand.

Johnny swung the musket into the back of her legs. She fell, face first, into the mud.

She twisted around to face him. He threw his musket aside and she scrabbled backwards. He leaned down and grabbed her leg, pulling her towards him; she kicked out wildly, catching his jaw with the heel of her boot. He yelped and let go.

She struggled back to her feet and ran, still clinging to the pistol.

She didn't have a plan. She wasn't thinking. She saw the door of the shed was padlocked. She didn't stop. She slammed into it hoping it would burst open. It didn't.

She turned to see Johnny, a mad giant, just yards away, running at her.

With her back to the shed door, she fumbled with the pistol, using her two thumbs to try to pull back the flintlock.

Johnny swung a punch, striking her in the side of the head. She was thrown to the ground.

Stunned, she blinked, trying to clear her vision. His great hulking shadow loomed above her, ready to strike again.

She pointed and fired.

TWENTY-ONE

She didn't know how long she lay there.

As she started to come to, she felt heavy, weighed down. She couldn't move, couldn't breathe.

She tried to force herself awake, force her eyes to open. She tried to remember where she was, what was going on. Her head was pounding, she was struggling to see, her arm stung and she felt weak.

There was a face close to hers; her focus cleared. It was Johnny, lying on the ground next to her. She was underneath him, underneath his leaden, unmoving weight. She tried to struggle against him, tried to move him. Desperately, she tried to wriggle free.

The breath was being forced from her chest by his sheer weight. She was panicking; she yelled in frustration.

She pushed down on his shoulders, desperately trying to move away from him.

Slowly, with all her might, she could slide her body out. She only had strength in her right arm, the left arm was numb. She sat up trying to pull her legs out from underneath him, trying to wriggle backwards, until finally first one and then the other leg was free. She fell back on the ground exhausted, breathing in the air, trying to fill her lungs once again.

She crawled onto her knees. Looking at the motionless body of the highwayman face down in the dirt. Her dress was drenched in his blood and her own. She was exhausted, and shaken. She had just killed a man. She never thought she would see this day, never had considered that such a possibility would exist. She didn't know if she should mourn him or revel in her victory. She didn't feel victorious.

Tentatively she touched the flesh on her arm, the wound had stopped bleeding it was sore, but didn't seem too deep.

Suddenly the remembered her father, she didn't know if he was safe, didn't know if Bess had managed to stop William.

Then she thought of Bess.

Bess had saved her father's life, and had risked her own to do so.

Suddenly Evelyn remembered a shot—it had come from the path.

She didn't know what had happened, she didn't know if William would be capable of shooting at his sister, if he had shot Bess.

She had to find out. She dragged herself onto her feet.

Unsteadily, she walked off through the woods heading toward the elm trees. She wasn't sure where William was. He could be in the woods, he could be behind the next tree, he may have already killed her father and he could be lying in wait for her, making sure he could take everything for himself. She didn't know, but she had to make sure, had to see for herself, that Bess was alright.

She had been so stupid to leave her at his mercy. He was mad, anything could have happened.

She reached the path and made her way out of the woods towards the lawn, she leaned on a tree, looking across the garden, uncertain as to whether it was safe.

Then she saw her, saw the red dress.

Evelyn ran forward. She didn't care about the pain; she ran through it, desperate to see. She needed to see for herself; she couldn't really believe it.

But there she was, lying on the ground.

Bess was pale. She looked asleep. She seemed so perfect.

Her hand was resting on her side, and Evelyn could see blood seeping from a tear in her red dress.

Evelyn couldn't breathe. She stared at her, unwilling to allow herself to believe what she saw.

Slowly she knelt on the ground and reached out, touching Bess' cheek. She was warm.

"Bess?" she asked, hoping against hope.

"Evie?" Her voice was weak barely audible, barely louder than a breath. But it was enough.

Evelyn reached forward grabbing her in her arms.

"Bess!" she gasped, "Bess! I thought you were dead! I thought you were gone! Stay with me!"

"Evie…" She slowly opened her eyes, looking up.

"It's alright. Everything is going to be alright."

"Billy…"

"He's gone. He's gone Bess."

"Your father."

"He's safe."

"No… William… He's gone after him."

"It doesn't matter!"

"He'll kill him, Evie."

"I shouldn't have left you. I should never have left you."

"Evie, please." She was reaching up to touch her face. "Please, you have to stop him."

"I can't leave you. I should never have left you. I was wrong, I was so wrong about you. I'm so sorry I doubted you."

Evelyn needed her to know, she needed to tell her that she believed in her and she was a fool to have ever thought differently.

Bess had been telling the truth since the very first night they were together. Everything she had done since that point she had done to help Evelyn, she had never betrayed her, never sought to hurt her, and had only ever wanted to help her.

She had tried to be loyal to her brother, but as soon as she was forced to decide between them, she had decided in Evelyn's favour.

Yet every time Evelyn had the slightest doubt she had assumed the worst of her, always throwing back in Bess' face everything she had fought so desperately to give, always making her work so hard to earn her trust. Time and time again, Bess had been loyal to her, but then the moment when it counted most of all, the moment when

Bess had needed Evelyn, she had run away. She had left her to die alone.

She couldn't leave her now. She couldn't leave her.

"Evelyn, you must…."

She was struggling to breathe and talk at the same time, and reluctantly Evelyn had to admit to herself that Bess was right. They both knew that at any moment William would come after them, he would kill her father, finish the job on Bess and then start on Evelyn. There was only one thing she could do.

She would have to fight.

It was up to her to save everyone and to do that she would have to leave Bess.

She looked down at her. Her skin was paler than ever, her eyes were drifting closed as she fought to stay conscious. Evelyn would have to leave her, but she had to let her know, had to tell her, what she had only just realised herself.

"I love you," she whispered.

Bess smiled and tried to reply, but she was gone. Her head rolled to the side. And Evelyn sobbed. She couldn't stay, she couldn't allow herself to fail, to collapse, she had to stop William. She had nothing else left to do.

Carefully she lay Bess' head on the ground and moved her onto her side. She tore some material from her skirts and held it over the wound, hoping the weight of Bess' arm would be enough to stem the flow of blood.

Then she left her.

She made her way around to the back of the house and in through the kitchens. She was expecting to see a roomful of people, all busying themselves with their duties, but the kitchen was eerily quiet. The table had been abandoned midway through cooking, it was dusted with flour and there was a dough left half kneaded: the cook had been ushered away from her post in a hurry.

Evelyn looked around the kitchen and found a large carving knife. She knew that William had fired his shot, she just hoped that he didn't have another.

She edged out of the kitchen all the time listening out for a voice, or a footstep, or the creaking of wood on the landing. Waiting to hear something and yet with every moment she was hoping that she wouldn't.

She sneaked along corridor and up the servant's steps. She had never known the house to be so quiet. On the one hand, she was relieved that they must have all rushed off to the village to raise a hue and cry, as well as escape from the villains. However, she wasn't sure if William had gone after them of if he was still prowling around the estate—by abandoning Bess, she may have put them both in danger. She promised herself that she would look around the house then go straight back to Bess and wait.

She opened the door leading out into the entrance hall, and looked through the small crack in the door, before opening it wider. There didn't appear to be anyone. Slowly, she crept out, brandishing her knife. Evelyn was aware that she may look rather frightening, creeping out of the kitchen covered in blood and brandishing a carving knife, she just hoped that she didn't frighten the life out of someone unintentionally. She had to press forward.

Silently, she tiptoed across the hallway, freezing as she walked across a creaky floorboard. She reached her foot out further and tried to step carefully beyond the board rather than making any more noise. She peered around the door of the dining room.

It was empty. Light spilled in through the windows, catching on the surface of the table. She thought about looking behind the curtains, but she couldn't bring herself to. She edged out of the room and closed the door, thinking that if anyone came out of that room she would hear the heavy door open.

She turned and went slowly towards the stairs; the front door was behind her. She knew that anyone could be waiting at the top of the stairs, or burst in behind her at the front door. She kept her back to the rail, and slid up the stairs sideways. Her stomach tightened as she crept slowly up each step, one after the other, slowly testing each stair for a creak before tentatively placing her whole bodyweight onto it.

She scanned the corridor at the top of the stairs, it didn't look as though there was anyone there, but she would have to look in each room, and she knew there were cupboards and wardrobes and then she thought of the attic. She was also aware that as she was going up the main stairs, William could well be on the opposite side of the house, going down the servant's stairs. They could creep around one another for hours.

If he was there.

If he was still in the house, if he hadn't followed the servants down to the village, and if he hadn't managed to rouse Jim from unconsciousness after his run-in with a shovel.

She hoped she was alone, she hoped she wouldn't find him, but she knew she had to keep looking, knew she had to do what she could to stop him from killing her father and the woman she loved. If they weren't already dead.

She crept down the corridor towards the study, sure

that if he was in the house, he would be there. Perhaps looking over papers, trying to work out how much he would own once he murdered them all, trying to work out how much of the estate he had already stolen and spent.

She was struggling to breathe as she neared the door. It was already slightly open, she glanced around, making sure that no one had appeared in the corridor, then, slowly, using the knife to push open the door, she peered in.

The room was empty, save Charlie, who still lay on the floor where he had fallen what seemed like hours ago. Evelyn wasn't sure if he was alive, she wasn't sure if she wanted to know, but she couldn't just leave his body on the floor of the study.

She checked again, making sure no one was hiding behind the door before creeping into the study, she knelt beside him and touched his cheek with the back of her hand, he was still warm. She breathed a sigh of relief and stood, turning to leave.

"Were you looking for me?"

TWENTY-TWO

He stood framed in the doorway. Evelyn backed away from him slowly.

She noticed he held his pistol in his hand. He was slowly stroking the flintlock with his thumb. She wasn't sure if it was the one he'd used on Bess, if it was loaded, or if it was empty.

"Yes," she managed to stammer, "I was looking for you. It's Bess—she's in a bad way… we'll have to call a doctor—"

He started towards her. His stride was strong, purposeful. She backed off and nearly tripped over the unconscious body of Charlie. William came right up to her, he started stroking her chin with the pistol, scrutinising her.

"I am not a fool, you know," he said carefully.

"I... I... know," she said. Her breathing was uneven.

Now that she had found him, she had no idea what she was going to do with him. She gripped the knife in her hand, unwilling to move. Even if she did plunge the blade into him, he may well just fire at her. All she had to do was to keep him here, keep him talking until her father and the servants came back to rescue her. They would call up the hue and cry, they would come to the house, they would rescue her, they would save Bess and then they would take William into custody.

But she didn't know when.

"I had everything so perfectly planned," he said. "It all hung together so perfectly, and then your damned father!" William turned away from her, striding across the room and leaning on the desk. "Your mad, bloody father!" he yelled, almost hysterical with laughter.

She held the knife tightly, perhaps she could make her move now, perhaps she could stab him now. In the back, while he talked, while he couldn't fire at her.

But even after everything she had been through, she was struggling to find the ability to kill him in cold blood. She couldn't do it. She just stood there limply, holding the knife, and thinking of Bess bleeding to death on the ground outside.

"What kind of a man asks for an investment?" She wasn't sure if he wanted a reply, "If I had just had the dowry everything would have been alright, if I had just had the dowry, that alone would have secured my debts." He turned to her. "Do you know how much I'm in debt?"

She shook her head slowly.

"Three thousand."

She gasped without thinking. Three thousand was enough to live comfortably for a year, even to keep a family and a small estate, how could one person amass so much money?

"And that is just what I have left to pay!" He laughed bitterly, then looked up at her. "You have no idea, do you?"

He started towards her again, and she backed off, edging towards the open door.

"You have no idea how much all this is worth, do you?"

She shook her head.

"You have no idea how many hours you would have to work, breaking your back in the fields, to pay for this suit, or just this waistcoat! You sit here in your pretty house, wearing your pretty dress, filling your head with nonsense from these useless books, while there are people not ten miles away starving in the gutter!" He shouted at her, his anger flaring in his cheeks, the spittle frothing at his mouth. "I will not be one of them!" he roared, pulling the flintlock back on his pistol. "I will not let you throw me in the debtor's hell hole so I can rot away, covered with disease-infested rats and crying out for death to come and fetch me. I will not have that!"

He pointed the pistol directly at her face. It was just a few inches away. She stared down the barrel, paralysed in fear. She had to do something—he was clearly mad—she had to do something to stop him. Her grip tightened on the carving knife, but he was too far from her; she'd missed her chance and now she was going to die, she was going to die on the floor of her father's study.

"Tell me where the deeds are for the house."

"I don't know!" She struggled to think, desperately thinking where they might be, but she didn't know. He shook the pistol at her, his face was manic, filled with rage and hate. She could no longer see even a trace of the Mr Barrington that she had known.

"WHERE ARE THEY?" he shouted at her.

"Try the drawer!" she was panicking. "The secret drawer, in the desk."

He looked at her for a second, then his face changed. He walked over to the desk and opened the top drawer, kneeling to look inside. She knew he could see the hidden drawer from where he was, but as he reached in to open it, she panicked.

She didn't know if the deeds were in there; she had no idea where they might be. She was frightened, and she knew she hadn't thought this through. She couldn't stay here, not locked in a room with this madman. As he reached in, opening the secret drawer, she turned and ran.

"EVELYN!" he shouted after her.

She sped down the corridor. She didn't know where she was going, she just had to run. She tore through the door at the end of the hall and up the flight of stairs to the servants' quarters. He was right behind her, calling after her. She tore down the hall, trying doors as she went.

They were locked. Everything was locked.

She had to keep running. She made a dash for another set of stairs at the end of the hall. She'd never even been to this part of the house. In all her time here, she had never even walked around the servant's quarters. She promised herself that in future she would explore every inch of every house she owned—she would know everything about it, including where the deeds were kept.

The stairs took her into a cramped attic space filled with old luggage trunks and furniture; there were spider webs and dust covering everything. The only light was through the dormer windows. They had been papered over, but some of the paper was falling off in places, allowing the light to pierce through.

She picked her way through the furniture. She could see a door at the other end, and she knew it would take her down again, it must take her down again, it had to.

"There's nowhere you can go!" William was behind her.

She turned to see him pointing the pistol at her. She still didn't know if it had been reloaded, she didn't know if she should take a chance. She was just a few feet from the door and the look on his face told her he would not be merciful with her even if she did as he said. She dived for the door. It was locked. She shook it desperately, hoping it was simply jammed.

"Get away from that door, Evelyn!" He was picking his way through the room after her.

She looked at him, her back to the wall, just the distance of fifteen feet between them. She couldn't stay. She turned to the window, unhooked the lock, and slid it open.

"Evelyn, NO!" he shouted after her.

She looked out of the window. It was four floors to the ground, and only the solid flagstone beneath. There was a foot or so of roof space before the solid drop. She didn't think twice. She held the carving knife in her left hand and swung out.

Tentatively, she edged along. Her shoes had very little to grip on the tiled roof and she knew she could easily slide off and down to the ground. She only had one free hand, and her left arm was searing with pain as she put weight on it to steady herself. But it was only a few feet up to the peak.

She held on to the roof of the dormer window and edged along, grabbing hold of the crux, and hauling herself up until her chest was level with it.

"Evelyn, get back here!" William was leaning out of the window to look up at her; she was out of his reach. If his gun was loaded, he would have fired it by now.

She scrambled upwards, struggling to get a foothold. It had looked like such a straight forward climb: just a shimmy across and then a leap up onto the crux. But stuck here, trying to haul herself onto the apex of the dormer, exhausted and in pain, she knew she could easily fall, and she understood the look of anxiety on William's face when finally, he swung himself out after her.

In desperation, she threw the carving knife at him; it missed by a long way, but her hand was free and, despite the pain, she could haul herself up on to the top of the dormer window. She clambered up delicately, and with her back to William she stood on top of the window and reached her arms up to the main crux of the house.

If she could just reach the main apex and haul herself over the ridge, she knew there was a flat space on the other side. She could run across it and back into the house. She just had to get over this ridge, but was just a few inches too far for her to reach.

Suddenly William grabbed her foot, and she screamed as he unsteadied her balance. She panicked, lashing out, and managed to strike him in the head with her boot. He yelled and slipped, only just grabbing hold of the window ledge to keep himself on the roof.

She looked up at the apex—just a few inches! If she jumped she could reach it, but if she slipped there was only solid stone to break her fall. She looked back down at William: he was even more determined to catch her and had started hauling himself back up towards her. She reached upwards, standing on the toes of one foot, giving herself an extra inch. It was just enough to edge her fingers around a tile; she clawed at it desperately.

It came loose in her hand. She looked at it in horror for a moment as William grabbed her foot once again. Without thinking, she threw the tile down at him. It hit him in the shoulder, causing him to let go of her momentarily. She regained her balance and reached up, yanking at another loose tile from the roof and throwing it down at him.

He yelled in rage as he deflected it with his hand. She pulled off another and another, pelting them at him with all the force she could muster. She had created a gap in the tiles; there was a wooden rail, she grabbed it, and gave herself the few extra inches she needed to get her hand and then her arm over the apex, hauling herself up until she was just out of his reach.

But William was right behind her, and he followed her route onto the dormer roof. She didn't have the strength to drag herself any further up; she couldn't pull herself over to the other side. In a panic, she started pulling at the tiles, throwing them down at him.

One of them landed square against his face—he lost his balance just for a second—and she launched another tile at him as he scrambled around trying to claw at something to hold him on.

He yelled as his body swung out. For a moment, she watched him. He seemed impossibly frozen in mid-air, his feet still on the dormer roof, but his hands flailing wildly, his face fixed in terror.

For that one moment, she wanted to reach out to him, to pull him back in, to save him from himself, to take back what she had done to him. But it was too late.

The weight of his body toppled him off the edge as his feet left the roof. His eyes were wide and full of life, but his death was already written.

Then he was gone.

She heard a crunch, and then silence. It was over.

TWENTY-THREE

She sat on the bench, allowing the last of the warm sun to touch her face before she went back up to the house. It was the first real chance she'd had to be alone over the last week.

Her arm still ached and the doctor had told her that the scars from the grape shot would stay with her forever, a constant reminder of what had happened. But then she thought back to William's face as he fell, the look of horror in his eyes and she realised that there would be other scars that would never heal.

It had been an exhausting week, one full of grief and stress. She'd never had to fight so hard for something. Even when fighting for her life, she'd not felt under so much pressure and scrutiny as when she was dealing with bureaucrats, the law, and the will of her father.

And she'd had to do it all alone.

But finally, this afternoon everything had been cleared, everything was arranged how she wanted it. She just hoped that it was somewhere close to how Bess would have arranged it all, had she been there to help.

She thought of Bess and her heart ached, she thought back to those few days when they had been together. She had felt so complete, so happy walking beside her, riding beside her and sleeping beside her. She hoped and prayed that she would feel that way again. She hoped that the last few days hadn't destroyed all hope of some kind of future.

She shivered.

The first chill of winter was in the air, autumn was on its way. The world was shifting. She looked at the garden, at the leaves turning brown, and she felt as though she too had changed. She would never be the same.

She would never be that bored, haughty little girl. Somehow, somewhere along the line that little girl had disappeared and rather than sitting back and watching the world drift wearily by, she felt as though she was a part of it, someone who can make a change, make a difference, carve out a place for herself and make something good happen in the world.

She stood and started back up the path towards her home.

The gap in the roof had already been fixed, but the workman's ladder was still there, still attached to the roof, the last hint that anything had taken place there, that anyone had even been up there.

The flagstone path below had been cleared long ago. The wreckage of a man's life, his hopes and dreams had come crashing to the ground in the same instant he fell from the rooftop.

His life had stopped and that had allowed Evelyn's life to finally start.

She walked past the flagstones and up to the house. She told herself that one day she would be able to walk past that place without dwelling on that moment. Either that or she would have to move, start a new life, and start afresh. Perhaps she could even travel or go to the New World, there was nothing stopping her, nothing holding her back. She was free to roam the earth should she so desire.

She hung her coat up and checked in on her father. He was sitting by the fire, his eyes closed, a book open on his chest and a glass of port beside him on the table.

She smiled. It was a relief to have him back to his old self: she remembered his haggard face, his desperately sorry frame. He had felt as though he had let her down, as though he should have protected her and looked after her, and that by not doing so, by not somehow preventing the sequence of events, that he had failed her.

But she had been able to show him that, far from failing in his duty as a father, he had given her resourcefulness, courage, and intelligence, and it was those gifts that had protected her when she needed them most. Now it would be her turn to look after him, to make sure that he was the one that was protected the way he had protected her when she needed it.

She carefully stepped over to him and removed the book from his chest, placing a bookmark in it and putting it on the side table. Then she left the room and headed up the stairs, glancing at the clock in the hall as she passed it.

There was plenty of time.

With her bad arm, she still found it a struggle to dress for dinner, but with the house back in order, and a lady's maid, she knew she would have time to spare.

She crept quietly down the hall, not wanting to disturb anyone. She opened the bedroom door quietly.

The curtains were drawn, letting in only a little of the fading light. The fire had been lit and the room felt warm and cosy. She closed the curtains and lit a few candles around the room to give herself some extra light, before sitting gently on the bed, beside Bess.

She was still asleep. She had barely been awake more than a few minutes since that day. The doctor had been careful to warn them that she wouldn't pull through and the parson had been called out more than a few times. Each time they had feared the worst, Evelyn had sat with her through the night, willing her to stay alive, willing her to stay with her just a few hours more.

In those long dark nights, she had thought, more than once, that she didn't deserve the happiness of seeing Bess alive again, and that it would be her punishment to realise and accept her love only to lose her so quickly.

But Bess had come through, she had stayed breathing, she had been able to eat a little each day, to keep her strength up, to keep alive, and she had been getting stronger.

It had taken all of Evelyn's talent and cunning, all her negotiation skills and persuasion, to keep Bess away from the hangman's noose. She was wanted in four counties, and had inherited her brother's debt.

Her father had been dubious and had, at first, refused to have anything to do with the girl. But slowly he had come around—she had been able to persuade him of her innocence, of her desire to help, of helping her to escape and, of course, the overriding factor was that she had taken a bullet intended for Mr Thackeray. Even he could not deny this.

That factor alongside their testimonies as character witnesses, and Evelyn's ability to lay the blame squarely on William and the other members of the gang, had ensured that Bess was a free woman. Evelyn just hoped that she would be alive to appreciate it

She slowly stroked her head. Bess was warm, but her temperature wasn't raging as it had been. Her skin was soft and pale against the dark black of her hair, and as Evelyn stroked her cheek she turned towards her and slowly opened her eyes.

Evelyn's heart stopped. Bess' eyes had fluttered open a few times over the week but she had never regained consciousness enough to recognise anyone or to talk any sense. But she looked up, her eyes darted about for a moment but then rested and focused on Evelyn.

She smiled and breathed out a slow sigh of relief.

"Bess?" Evelyn said slowly, hoping that she would finally hear the response she craved.

"Evie?" said Bess weakly. She struggled to sit up.

"No, no, no," Evelyn said, gently holding her down. "Stay as you are, you still need a lot of rest."

"Where am I?" she asked, looking around.

"You're in my house, the guest room. My room is just next door."

"What happened?"

"What do you remember?"

Bess looked away for a moment, she was distant as if replaying the last memories over in her mind. Her eyes widened.

"Bill!" she said, "Bill, he's gone after your father, you must stop him."

She tried edging out of the bed as if to go on the hunt herself.

"Shh," Evelyn said, stopping her from leaving. "It's over, it's all over, that was all days ago."

"Days?" Bess looked up at her, anxious.

"You've been in here nearly a week—we thought we had lost you a few times, but you were so strong."

Bess lay back on the bed and looked at Evelyn. She still seemed anxious.

"What happened?"

Evelyn took a deep breath. She had been trying to forget the events of that day, and she didn't want to re-live them.

"Jim and Charlie were taken away and charged. Jim has been sentenced to transportation, but Charlie has some good character references, so he may go free if he can pay the fines."

"And Bill?" asked Bess, looking up at her.

She took a breath, trying to find the words to explain what she had done.

"He didn't make it," she said finally.

Bess nodded; her face was firm. She had known that outcome would happen eventually and she had been ready for it.

"And your father?" she asked

"He is alright, he managed to get to the village with the servants, they were able to set off the hue and cry, bringing in the local guard and fetching the doctor. The village still hasn't overcome the excitement of it all. In fact, I'm not sure they ever will."

But there was still something bothering Bess. She looked up at Evelyn.

"And me?" she asked, "Am I to be –"

"No," said Evelyn, cutting her off before she could even suggest anything. "Your name has been cleared, I made sure of that. Everything that happened has been laid squarely on your brother's shoulders."

"Poor Bill," she said sadly.

Evelyn's stomach twisted in guilt, as she thought perhaps she had done the wrong thing, perhaps Bess would always blame her for her brother's death, and for tarnishing his name with her crimes.

"He was so filled with hate; he would never have been at peace, even with all the money in the world, he would still have felt he had been wronged."

"I'm so sorry he's gone," Evelyn said, holding Bess' hand.

Bess looked up at her and smiled.

"What else could have been done?" she asked. "He chose a path without a future."

Evelyn breathed deeply—she knew Bess was right, but it was still a relief to hear her say the words. She stroked her head.

"I should bring you up some food. You need to build up your strength."

"Thank you," Bess said, gently squeezing her hand.

"That's alright, you need to eat."

"No, thank you for saving me, for clearing my name. I don't know how I can ever repay you."

"Stay," Evelyn whispered. She wanted it more than she had ever wanted anything. "Stay with me, here in this house, or another house, I don't care, just say that you'll stay with me and never leave."

"But what about—"

"I'll take care of everything. You won't have to worry about anything or anyone, just say that you'll stay with me, because I don't think I could bear to live without you. I love you."

Bess smiled, and grasped her hand tighter.

"I love you too."

"So, you'll stay?" Evelyn felt desperate.

"Of course," she said. "I wouldn't want to be anywhere else."

THE END

REVIEWS ARE EVERYTHING!

Readers who take the time to write reviews are **precious**, not everyone can and not everyone will.

But reviews mean everything to a writer!

I love hearing your thoughts, what you liked, what you think could have been different and why other people should follow in your footsteps and take a chance on this story.

So now you have finished this anthology, please take the time to share a few words about it on Amazon.

Help someone else find a story they'll cherish.

Niamh Murphy

ALSO BY THE AUTHOR

ESCAPE TO PIRATE ISAND

You can't run away from yourself...

The year is 1720 and two young women are about to find themselves in more trouble than they could ever have imagined possible.

Cat Meadows is a smuggler who's built her reputation on the backs of unsuspecting souls.

Lily Exquemelin has been left nothing by her father but his troubles and his treasure map.

Forced to make a desperate escape, they each find themselves on a Trans-Atlantic adventure that will pit them against pirates, mutineers, lost treasure, and each other!

Can they learn to trust one another and escape the clutches of their would-be captors or will their past's finally catch up to them?

Find out in this swashbuckling, romantic adventure!

MAGIC AND ROMANCE
A COLLECTION OF LESBIAN SHORT STORIES

A cross-genre anthology of Sapphic tales.

Including Mask of the Highwaywoman, the short story that inspired Niamh's debut novel.

If you like reading about vampires, werewolves, ballroom dancing, student-life, historical romance, or even epic fantasy, all with a twist of lesbian romance and a dash of action and adventure then you will love this exciting and funny anthology by Niamh Murphy.

GRETEL: A FAIRYTALE RETOLD

Once in a while, love gives us a fairytale...

Tormented by a pack of bloodthirsty wolves, Hans, and his sister Gretel, run for their lives.

Desperation leads them into the comforting arms of a beautiful woman whom asks for nothing in return for her kindness.

As their friendship blossoms, Gretel finds herself drawn to the seductress, while Hans grows suspicious of her motives.

Torn between the brother she adores and the woman she can't help but admire, Gretel is forced to make a choice.

Will sibling bonds override the lure of a newfound love?

Gretel: A Fairytale Retold is a six-chapter novella of over 12,400 words.

Niamh Murphy

ABOUT THE AUTHOR

Niamh Murphy is a historian and novelist specialising in romantic lesbian fiction. In 2012, she published her debut novel 'Mask of the Highwaywoman', a swashbuckling historical romance that combined her love of history and adventure. She went on to complete an MA in creative writing at the University of Essex in 2016 and is now working on putting all her fantastical stories on the page.

She is passionate about experimenting with different genres and has a fondness for romantic action and adventure. She has written stories with vampires, werewolves, elves, magic, knights, sorceresses, and witches as well as contemporary and humorous stories, but always with a lesbian protagonist and a romantic element to the tale.

She currently lives in the historic town of Colchester, England, where she can indulge her passion for archaeology and history. Her greatest ambition is to own a medieval castle, complete with turrets, towers, a moat, and a drawbridge.

Niamh Murphy

Made in the USA
Middletown, DE
16 April 2018